ZANE AND THE HURRICANE

A STORY OF KATRINA

Also by
RODMAN PHILBRICK

ZANE AND THE HURRICANE

A STORY OF KATRINA

RODMAN PHILBRICK

SCHOLASTIC INC.

Copyright © 2014 by Rodman Philbrick

This book was originally published in hardcover by The Blue Sky Press in 2014.

All rights reserved. Published by Scholastic Inc., *Publishers since 1920.* SCHOLASTIC and associated logos are trademarks and/or registered trademarks of Scholastic Inc.

The publisher does not have any control over and does not assume any responsibility for author or third-party websites or their content.

ISBN 978-0-545-34239-1

10 9 8 7 6 5 4 3 2 1   15 16 17 18 19

Printed in the U.S.A.   40
First printing 2015

Book design by Jeannine Riske
Maps by Jim McMahon

In loving memory of
Lynn Harnett, 1950–2012

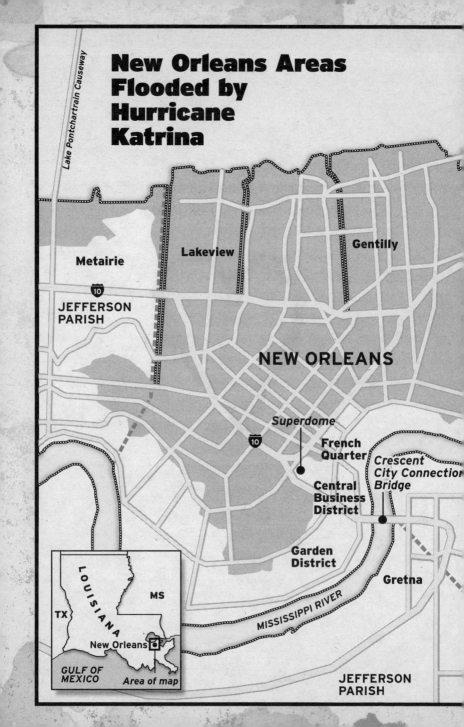

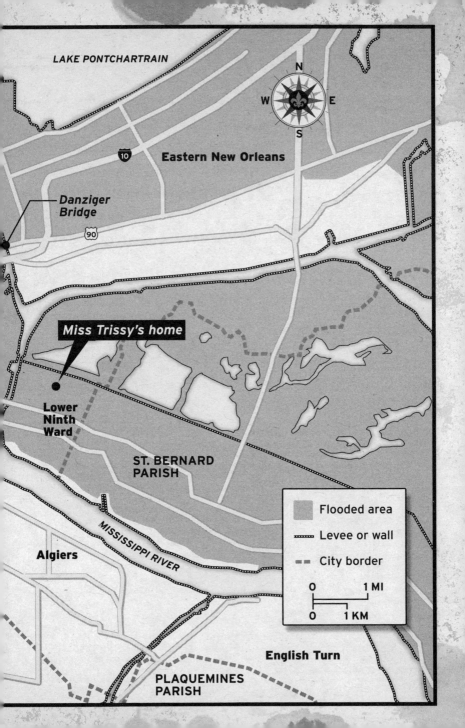

1.

My Stupid Trip to Smellyville

Bandy is a mutt like me. He's black and white and small enough to hide in a gym bag, except he can't keep from barking *hi-hi-hi* with his silly tongue hanging out and his little tail sticking up. Bandy, short for Bandit, because of the black marking across his eyes and nose. Don't get me wrong, he's the best dog in the world, and what happened wasn't really his fault, even if it nearly got me killed two times. Three if you count the tippy canoe. Later on he made up for it by totally saving my life. Of course none of it would have happened if my mom didn't make me visit the golden oldies in Smellyville, which is what I called New Orleans before I knew better. Before the wind and the rain and the flood, and me having to pretend I was brave, even though inside I was scared to death.

My name is Zane Dupree. I need to warn you right now, there's some really gross stuff in this book, and I'm not talking about make-believe gross like plastic poop and vomit, but stuff so awful it made a dog hide his nose, and believe me Bandy will sniff at most anything. Other than dog food, his favorite smells are dirty socks and toilet bowls, so that should give you an idea how bad things got.

Okay, deep breath, back to the beginning. How it started, me going to New Orleans. If you don't already know, summers are pretty great in New Hampshire, where I live. The sky is blue and clear and the days last almost forever.

This one perfect summer morning Bandy and me are out in the yard fooling around for a while. Playing this game where he tries to guess where I'm going to throw his ball, which I do with my eyes closed, and most of the time he guesses right and is waiting there before the ball hits the ground. Mom says me and Bandy have some kind of boy-dog mind-meld thing, like we can read each other's thoughts. I don't know about that, but for sure that little dog seems to know what I'm going to do before I do, which is maybe kind of weird but also really cool.

Anyhow, when we come back inside that perfect summer day my mom is sitting in the kitchen with the phone on the table and her eyes all red.

"Did somebody die?" I ask, because that's how she looks.

"No, no. Nothing like that," she says, sniffing back a tear. "The opposite. Somebody I didn't think could possibly still be alive."

Oh yeah, I forgot to mention about my father dying before I was born. Mom and him met when they were in the Air Force, and then they got married and moved to New Hampshire and started a new family — me. My dad happened to be in the wrong place at the wrong time. Some old gumby had a stroke and ran him over.

For the record I really hate it when people feel sorry for me because my father is dead. It's too bad he died and everything, but I never knew him so I never missed him, okay? Because you can't miss somebody you never knew, can you?

Anyhow, back to my mom. She's all weepy because she finally managed to locate one of my father's long-lost relatives.

"Her name is Beatrice Jackson. They call her Miss Trissy. She's your great-grandmother and from what she told me she pretty much raised your father. In New Orleans, Louisiana."

"New Orleans? You said he was from Mississippi."

She nods. "That's what he always told me. Biloxi, Mississippi. Didn't ever have much to say about his family, or what happened in the years before we met, but Gerald was living in Biloxi when he enlisted in the Air Force, I always knew that for sure, it's right there on his induction form. So when he — when the accident happened, I called every Dupree in the book down there. My own father, bless him, he even hired a local investigator. But it was a dead end. Never could find any of your dad's relatives in the state of Mississippi. We thought they were all gone."

"You already told me that stuff like a bunch of times," I say, dropping into a kitchen chair.

Mom gives me this pleading look. "Don't be angry at me, Zaney. You'll be thirteen on your next birthday and I thought you should know something about your father. Whatever there is to know. Something besides photographs and me with my stories. So I tried this new website for connecting families and what do you know, it worked."

"Okay fine," I say, making a bored face. "So now I know. There's an old lady with a funny name that used to know my father."

"Raised him! She raised him!" Mom says, excited and talking fast. "She's your blood, honey. From what I can tell, she's all that's left, and she never even knew you existed until she picked up the phone this morning. She sounds really lovely, and very old, of course, and more than anything in the world she wants to see you before . . . you know."

"Before she dies."

"Don't say that."

"It's what you mean, isn't it?"

"Zaney, listen to me," she pleads. "This is important, okay? We need to get this right."

Fine. Whatever. At first I figure the old lady will visit us in New Hampshire and I'll have to be nice and everything, but it turns out she's too old to travel, and since Mom can't get time off from work she thinks I should go down there on my own.

By myself. Without Bandy.

"Totally no way," I say, folding my arms. "Never going to happen. Never, never, never."

Never is a bad word to use on my mom. She also hates it when I say "totally no way." She's never hit me, not ever in my whole life, but that day we have a big yelling fight that ends with her slamming her bedroom door. I can hear her sobbing, which totally ruins everything because it wrecks me when she cries. Maybe it isn't cool to say this, but she's the best mom in the world and I'd never on purpose make her cry. Are we clear on that? Good. So eventually we come to an agreement: if the old lady lets me bring Bandy I'll agree to visit her for the last week of summer.

To call that bad timing would be, as Mom later said, the understatement of the century. Because I fly down to New Orleans on a Monday in late August. The very next day something called a tropical depression forms near the Bahama islands, almost a thousand miles away. A day later they give the storm a name. They call it Katrina, and it's coming to get us, but we don't know that then.

We don't know much, me and Bandit the Wonder Dog. All we know is we don't want to be there.

2.

What the Old Lady Said

The truth is, when me and Bandy first get off the plane and this old lady is waiting there with her two canes, one in each fist, I'm kind of scared of her. She's so wicked old and the canes look like weapons. Like hitting sticks. This really ancient lady, small and hunched with her hitting sticks. Her skin like the skin on milky hot chocolate when you blow across the top, all wrinkled and folded back on itself. Even her perfume smells like old flowers or something.

More than anything I want to get back on the plane and go home, but then the old lady says something that changes my mind, at least a little bit. Standing there kind of wobbly on her canes but smiling like the sun peeking through a cloud, she goes, "Young man? Seems I been waiting all my life to meet you, though I didn't know you existed, or what yo name might be. The Good Lawd has given me a great gift. Thank you Lawd! Praise be! Zane Dupree, you are welcome in my home today and always will be. Mmm, mmm, mmm."

You can't be afraid of a person who says that. You just can't. Plus Bandy likes her — right away he rolls over and shows her his tummy, so that's another thing in her favor.

"Hello to you, too," she says, scratching behind his ears with the tip of her cane. "Let me guess, this dog part terrier and the rest nobody quite sure, is that about right?"

"Yes, ma'am," I say.

"Can you drag your bag and that little dog, too? Taxicab waitin' on us."

When we first walk out of that terminal into the heat of the city it's like whoa, are they kidding? This has to be a joke. I've never been anywhere that's so unbelievably hot and humid. Like the sky is sweating and everything smells kind of stinky and moldy and wet.

That's when I start to think of New Orleans as Smellyville. I didn't know it then, but the wet and stinky part was about to get much, much worse.

3.

Older than Dirt

Okay, that's settled, how me and Bandit happened to be in New Orleans when the hurricane hit. The other thing you should probably know is, I'm what they sometimes call biracial or multiracial or whatever. White mother, black father, okay? Except if you go back to everybody who came before me there's way more than two races. There's African and English and Saxon and Celts and Creole and Cherokee, and that's just for starters. I bet there's even some Chinese ancestors if you go back far enough.

Turns out Trissy Jackson has strong opinions on the subject of race and color. "Multiracial? Naw, that don't say it. That don't get the true flavor. You of mixed race, boy," she says, studying my face and humming to herself, which she does all the time. "Yup, you mixed, same as me. Let me explain. My daddy was a light-skinned Negro, call him 'high yaller' in his day — that was a insult — but he did think very high of himself, come to that. See, one of my daddy's grandfathers was white and his own momma was a Creole of color, which is partly African blood and partly French blood, descended by way of the free people of color. A whole class of they own. So you all kinds mixed together. But it don't matter who was my daddy's people, my daddy was colored because African blood made you colored, even if half yo ancestors was white. Mmm, mmm. Them was the rules. Them was the laws. Sounds complicated, I know, but in the day we all knew what was what, who was who."

"Hardly nobody says 'colored' now," I point out, in case she doesn't know, being so old.

"I just did," she says, and laughs. "For your information 'colored' was a polite word back then, when I'm speaking of, when I was a little girl. Long, long time ago. You and me, we gotta lot of catchin' up. All your life and some that came before. Oh my, yes. From the look of you, yo momma's got true blond hair, that 'bout right?"

I nod.

"And you gots her straight hair, mostly, 'cept yours is darker hair. See, hair is what folks see first. Folks don't know no better might glance at you and see only the white part, on account yo hair. White boy with freckles and thick straight hair and them green eyes. Oh, but I see Gerald in you, too, yes I do. Gerald's chin, Gerald's skinny nose, Gerald's freckles. You got his same mischiefy look about you and that's a fact. Oh, oh, Lawd have mercy, yo daddy looking at me from outta yo face, yes he do. No doubt, no doubt, mmm, mmm, mmm."

The humming, the mmm, mmm, it isn't regular humming, it's more like church singing. Hymns. Miss Trissy still sings in the church choir every Sunday, even if it takes two canes to get her there. She says she has the voice of a much younger woman and I'm to go to church with her this coming Sunday so I can hear it for myself.

"Much younger," she insists, proudly. "My singin' voice so young it still go out dancin' on Sat'day night. There, I made you smile."

When I say Miss Trissy is wicked old, I don't mean she's wicked like a bad person, because she's the opposite of that. I just mean really really old. I ask how old, exactly, which apparently is an impolite question, and she leans on her canes and gives out a little snort and goes, "Zactly? Zactly is it? I tell ya zactly. I'm zactly older than dirt, chile, and that's all ya need to know," and then she softens up and explains how it's bad luck to brag about her age because the Good Lawd might be listening and have cause to remember that she's long past her sell-by date.

"Ya got no idea what that means, do ya, young Mr. Dupree? I can see by yo face ya don't. Sell-by date is what dey stamp on a caw-tun of milk. Sell-by such and such a date because after that it go bad."

"So you've gone bad?" I ask, trying to be funny.

"Oh, you a terrible child," she says, but her eyes are smiling. "Terrible, terrible. Most of me gone bad, and that's the troot!"

Bandy's ears perk up whenever he hears her voice, especially when she laughs. And he likes it when she scratches his tummy with the tip of her cane.

"You understand what we speaking of?" she says to him. "Ears that big, you don't miss a thing. Oh! You a good one, you."

Miss Trissy has a story about everything in her little white house. How the rug in the hallway came from Algiers — not the city in Africa, but a neighborhood in New Orleans where her father had a store. And how the glass figurines on the shelf in the dining room came from her mother, who collected them, and the bowling trophy on top of the TV set is from her second husband, Henry, that died thirty years ago. There are lots of framed pictures on the wall, and a drawer full of loose photographs, most of them really old. She shows me a small, faded snapshot of two boys about my age. They have their arms around each other's shoulders and they look real happy.

"They come into my care after their momma passed. This yo daddy," she says, touching one of the boys with her thumb. "James was his little brother, by less than a year. They both in heaven now."

I ask why my father ran away from home.

"I expect he had his reasons," she says, not meeting my eyes.

"So his brother would have been my uncle, right?"

"Had he lived, uh-huh, but he passed before you born."

"What happened?"

"James got hissef killed, like so many other young mens." The old woman shakes her head, eyes brimming with tears. "Later child. We talk on that bye and bye."

Fine by me. I was only asking because I thought she'd expect me to. "Got hissef killed," though. Hear that and you can't help wondering. If it was an accident, like happened to my dad, wouldn't she say "died in an accident"? "Killed" sounds like somebody killed him, which makes me wonder how it happened, and who did it, and like that.

But Trissy changes the subject. "So yo momma got her a job with the US Post Office. That good," she says, sounding bright and cheerful again. "That a fine thing."

"My father did, too," I tell her. "He was delivering mail when he got run over by the old — by the person that hit him."

"Uh-huh, yo momma said. Terrible thing. Terrible. By any chance do you like ice cream? There's ice cream in the freeze box. Myself, I love ice cream."

That's another thing I like about the old lady. When she wants to change the subject she usually mentions ice cream.

4.

Fly Like Superman

When I was little, me and Mom went on vacation to a bunch of theme parks in Florida. One of the coolest rides was called "Back to the Future" and I liked it even though I hadn't seen the movie yet, which I did as soon as we got home. It's about this kid that goes back in time before he was born and tries to stop bad stuff from happening to his parents. A totally cool idea, even if it can't happen in real life.

Anyhow, that's what it's like at Miss Trissy's house, like the airplane that took me to New Orleans went back in time, and everything is from fifty years ago. Her little kitchen is clean and shiny, but the appliances could be out of a museum, if they had a museum about old kitchens. The telephone is this big black thing with a rotary dial instead of buttons, and a receiver so heavy she has to lift it with both hands. The old tube-model TV only gets one blurry channel because Miss Trissy doesn't have cable. Mostly she listens to gospel songs on an old table radio and sings along, which sounds kinda stupid but is actually sort of beautiful, once you get used to it.

The other thing that's like going back in time is that she doesn't have AC. Air-conditioning might as well never have been invented, as far as Miss Trissy is concerned. She doesn't believe in it, says air-conditioning will give you wetness of the lungs.

"That's what made me a widow," she says. "Wet lungs took my poor husband Henry."

I almost say it was probably the heat killed her husband, but I don't have the energy to smart-mouth. That's how hot it is. And that's mostly what I remember about the first three days in Smellyville. The heat that never stopped. How it was too hot to go outside in the daytime because the sun would hit you like a hot fist. I took Bandy out for his walks, of course, but we never went much farther than the empty lot at the end of the street because he'd whimper from the heat and want me to carry him back into the shade. Mostly he wanted to lie on his belly on the linoleum in the kitchen and pant and give me looks like the weather was all my fault.

"Nothing I can do about the temperature, you silly dog. Want a treat? Does that help?"

It usually does.

In the evening, when it was a little cooler, we'd sit out on the wooden porch they call a "gallery" and drink sweet iced tea and Miss Trissy would tell stories from the old days, about when my father and his brother were little and they played Superman in this very yard.

"That was they favorite — Superman, because he could fly. Don't matter he was a white man, them two wanted to be

Superman just the same. They tie towels around their necks for capes and stand on the gallery rail and make whooshing noises like they was flying. Gave me fits! What if they fell off and broke they heads? Couldn't stop 'em, though. They was determined to be Superman, and when Henry, he my husband at that time, when Henry say there only one Superman, how can you both be Superman, they say Superman can be anything he wants, even two people. They was that close, them two. Peas in a pod."

I keep waiting for her to tell me what happened, how my uncle James got killed and why my father ran away, but she never quite gets to that part.

"Bye and bye," she says, "bye and bye."

That's mostly all we do, really, is sit around and talk, because Miss Trissy is so old she doesn't like to leave the house except to go to church. The true fact is, even though she turns out to be nice and all, it's really pretty boring with no games and no TV, and I'm thinking only a few more days and this will be over and then school starts, which I'm sort of looking forward to, even though I'd never admit it to anyone.

Saturday morning the old phone rings. Bandy starts barking and I'm shushing him when Miss Trissy hands me the receiver and says, "Oh my Lawdy. Yo momma, child."

Mom calls my cell phone every day, usually in the morning, and for the past couple of days she's been concerned about this hurricane out in the Atlantic somewhere, which was supposed to be over once it hit Florida, but the weather channel has got her all riled up. Something about a bull's-eye.

"I tried your cell but it won't go through! Too many calls, I guess, which is no surprise. The storm track changed! The storm didn't die out like they thought. It came back to life when it crossed over Florida and hit that warm water in the Gulf. It got big — really big and now it's a huge big storm, aiming straight for New Orleans. They say the storm surge might be twenty feet high! High enough to flood the whole city! You got to leave, Zaney. You and Miss Trissy, you've got to get out of there!"

I explain that Miss Trissy doesn't have a car, but of course Mom already knows. She has a plan, which is totally typical because my mom always has a plan.

"You're coming home," she tells me. "You and Miss Trissy both. All you have to do is get to the airport. Can you do that?"

5.

Rise Up and Go

Going home a few days early seems like a great idea to me, even if we had to blame it on a hurricane. New Hampshire won't be as hot and muggy as New Orleans, that's for sure. And home has a real TV and my PlayStation and I'll have my friends and Bandy will have all the familiar places where he sniffs around and does his business. Plus I won't have to feel guilty about Miss Trissy because she's coming with us. That way Mom can deal with the old lady while I'm getting ready to go back to school.

Perfect. Selfish, maybe — okay, totally selfish — but I'm so psyched about going home that I get my stuff packed in like five minutes and carry it out to the porch — excuse me, the gallery — and check with Miss Trissy to make sure she's called for a taxi.

"Take 'em an hour at least to fetch us," she explains. "They busy."

She's at her little telephone table in the hallway and her hands are kind of fluttering around, like she's trying to touch invisible things. She always looks old but now she looks kind of sick, too.

"What's wrong, Grammy?"

Her ancient, wrinkled eyes are wet with tears. "Nice you call me 'Grammy.' Oh my yes, just like your father. Did you know that? That your daddy called me 'Grammy'? Course you didn't."

"But why are you crying?"

"The stoam," she says, which is her way of saying *storm*. "Already worried my way through that Hurricane Dennis that barely missed us, and now comes along this Katrina. One after another. You get settled from one stoam they comes another. Stoams gonna be the end of me."

"No, no, don't worry. We'll be fine. You're gonna love New Hampshire, Grammy, promise! Come on, sit down in your favorite chair and rest until the taxi gets here."

I help her settle into the easy chair but her hands are shaking so bad she loses her grip and the canes skitter to the floor, which sets the dog to barking.

"Bandy! Hush!"

"Ain't the wind I'm feared of," she explains. "It the water. Water take all this away, like Betsy did, and leave me no place to live in my last years."

"Betsy?"

"Hurricane of 1965. Forty years ago it flood this house up to the windowsills. Rising water drove us up into the attic. Imagine me climbing through that little hole in the ceiling? Well, I did!

Had to! My husband Henry brung him a little hatchet in case we had to chop through the roof. Then the water went back down, and we never did need that hatchet, but we was cleaning out and fixing up for the most part of a year, after that stoam, me and Henry. Don't got it in me to go through nothing like that again."

I say, "On TV they always make it sound worse than it is. Probably it'll blow down a few trees, that's all."

The old woman shakes her head sorrowfully. "We can't know that, child. Nobody knows but the Lawd, and He not sayin'."

Right about then my cell phone rings. Mom again, but the connection is so bad I can barely hear her.

"There's a problem," she says, her voice all crackly and distant.

The call fades away into static, but not before she gives me the bad news.

The really bad news.

Grammy goes, "What's wrong, child? Look like you ate a bug."

There's a lump in my throat not because I'm afraid of the storm — which is probably stupid — but because the promise of going back early has been snatched away, and it makes me more homesick than ever. "Delta canceled our flight," I finally manage to explain. "They canceled all flights for the next few days. Mom is trying to get us on standby with another airline, but so far she can't get through."

The old woman doesn't seem the least bit surprised. She hums to herself for a while and then gives me a big smile and goes, "You said it yourself, Zane Dupree. We gone be okay."

"I guess."

"Today is Saturday and the stoam don't be comin' till Monday soonest, right?"

"That's what they say."

"So we got all of Sunday," Grammy says. "Here's what we gone do. Tomorrow morning we go to church and see what da Lawd provide."

I must have walked past the New Mission Zion Baptist a bunch of times with Bandy and didn't even notice the place because at a glance it looks like the rest of the houses in the neighborhood. Just another long narrow building with white clapboards and a saggy front porch. But if you look closer there's a little wind-vane kind of steeple tacked onto the peak of the roof, and a hand-lettered sign is set out on the sidewalk that says *Worship with the Reverend W. B. Daniels, Jr., Pastor, Special Service Today 11:00 a.m.* and under that, *Sunday School Canceled.*

Grammy walks to church on her two canes and won't let me help her. She's made me put on my only white shirt and an old tie that belonged to Henry and smells of mothballs. She doesn't approve of my Nikes, but I don't have any dress shoes with me and her husband's old shoes don't fit, so the Nikes will have to do. Still, she's all got up in a blue satin dress, and what she calls her church shoes, and a wig that looks kind of purple, and a lacy blue hat on top of the wig. Sounds funny when I tell it like that, with the wig and all, but somehow she looks right, like a proper old lady on Sunday morning, all fixed up for church.

A man in a dark suit stands on the steps outside the church, looking up and down the street and checking his watch. He's a big dude with shiny dark skin and friendly eyes and gold-rimmed reading glasses that hang on a cord around his neck. When he catches sight of us his face lights up. "Miss Trissy! Welcome. Wasn't sure to see you this morning of all mornings," he says, leaning down to kiss her cheek. "Many of our parishioners have already gone."

"I come to sing for my great-grandchild I never knew I had," she says all in a burst, like she's been saving it up and has to get it out fast.

As the pastor shakes my hand he sort of looks me over, then back and forth between me and my great-grandmother. Finally he goes, "You know what? I do see it. Yes, I do, in the eyes and nose. Can you sing, too, young Mr. Dupree? Did the gift pass to you?"

I shake my head.

"Might be he does sing," Grammy says, smiling at me.

No way am I going to sing in church and make a fool of myself.

Totally no way.

Okay, try going to church in New Orleans and not singing. They won't let you. It's practically against the law not to sing in church there. It starts right off the bat, too. Pastor Daniels reads a few lines of scripture and then he turns to a keyboard set up alongside the podium, and as soon as his fingers touch the keys the whole room is singing this old-fashioned hymn about storm clouds and strong winds and finding the Savior and how sweet He is. The pastor, he's got a big voice that fills the place, and soon we're all kind of swaying back and forth in our seats and you don't even have to know the words, they're already there in the air, waiting for you to sing them.

Then at the end of the first chorus the pastor sets off a drum machine, changing the beat, and suddenly that old hymn turns into a stomping blues-rock kind of thing, and that's when Grammy stands up in the pew and opens her mouth. What comes out really floors me. Because she's got this clear, uplifting voice that's almost as big as the pastor's, a voice so young and beautiful it makes you want to cry and laugh at the same time, coming out of a little old lady like that.

Everybody in the church is clapping together — *clap! dah-dah-dah clap! dah-dah-dah clap!* — and swaying from side to side, shouting out, "Tell the Lord, Miss Trissy!" and singing like an echo on the chorus, and it's enough to make me want to jump out in the aisle and start dancing like a maniac, which of course I don't. I just clap along and maybe sing a little bit, keeping kind of quiet so nobody will notice my froggy voice that keeps missing notes. Not that anybody does notice, and the nice thing is that when the hymn is over my great-grandmother takes my hand and holds it like something precious, and that's when I really understand how cool it is that Mrs. Beatrice Jackson is still alive in the world for me to know, even if it meant coming all the way to Smellyville to find her.

After the one song Pastor Daniels calms us down and leads us to say the Lord's Prayer and then he thanks us all for coming and tells us this will be the end of the special service. Because the time has come to leave. "I pray we will all be in attendance next Sunday, and that the sun will be shining and that no harm will have come to us, or this ward, or our little church, but you heard me right, brothers and sisters, you all must go now. This very morning the mayor has issued a mandatory evacuation! They called most every church and every pastor to make sure the word gets out. They saying the hurricane may push a great wave of water, overtopping the levees and flooding the city, and some of you are old enough to recall the last time it happened, when much of our Lower Ninth neighborhood was flooded. We pray that this hurricane passes us by, as so often they do, and that our Lord's merciful hand will calm the waters so harm comes to no one. But brothers and sisters, make no mistake. We must take action as well as lift our voices in prayer. We must lift ourselves from these pews and go out and find transportation. Pack your bags and leave! Lock your doors and leave! Go to family, go to friends, but go you must. Bad winds are coming, brothers and sisters, and the waters may rise. Get thee to higher ground. Go, go, go!"

That does it. The church empties until there's no one left but me and Grammy and the pastor.

"Is there no one to carry you?" he asks.

The old woman shakes her head.

"Best come with me," he says. "We'll make room in the bus."

6.

Dumb and Dumber

An hour later we're on the highway, stuck in traffic and barely moving. What the pastor calls his "church bus" is really more like a passenger van with extra seats in the back. And no AC — he says running the AC will overheat the old engine — and we're jammed in there with nine people plus tons of luggage.

Nine people plus Bandit. At first the pastor didn't want to take a pet along, but Grammy insisted the dog was part of the family and couldn't be abandoned, no more than a child could be left behind, and the pastor relented. Bandy is curled up on my lap, trying to behave himself.

We've got the windows rolled down but there's no breeze — wouldn't you know it with a hurricane on the way? — and it looks like the whole city of New Orleans is stuck on the same on-ramp with us, even though every single lane of the highway is heading north.

"They call it 'contraflow,'" Pastor Daniels explains.

"Supposed to make it faster to evacuate. What that really means is no turning back!"

We're headed for Baton Rouge and will be given shelter at another church where Pastor Daniels's cousin is the preacher. He says it'll be an adventure and we'll all learn something, but I'm still wishing I could just go home. Last time I talked to Mom she was trying to look on the bright side and said it was for the best, evacuating to Baton Rouge, and that I'd get to meet all kinds of new people.

Sorry, but I don't want to meet new people, okay? I know that's mean and awful and ungrateful and everything, but I'd rather be in my own house, just me and Mom and Bandy.

So there I am, all stuffy and sweaty from the heat and feeling sorry for myself, when this big SUV with dark tinted windows edges along next to us. Can't be a foot away, with a big engine growling. I bet they got the AC on. I bet they do. And then one of the dark windows slides down a few inches and these sleek, nasty Dobermans poke their heads out and start barking and snarling. Vicious kind of snarling, like they can't wait to shred something to pieces. Something small and alive, like the little dog in my lap.

I should have known what would happen, soon as I saw the black gleam of those Doberman eyes. I should have clung to Bandy like my life depended on it, which — as it turns out — it did. But everything happens so fast. One second Bandit is curled in my lap, the next he leaps clear across the van and out the opposite window, as far away as he can get from those snarling Dobermans.

"Bandy!"

I shout for him, but the way he exploded out of the van I know he's not coming back as long as those Dobermans are barking. And now they're barking worse than ever, slavering and biting at the window glass, trying to chew their way out of the SUV to chase after Bandy.

As for me, I'm in a panic yelling stuff like, "Stop! Please stop the van!" and "Turn around, we have to go back!"

The pastor stares at me in the rearview mirror, shaking his head. "Can't stop, boy. Everything headed north, like it or not. We got the traffic inching up on us from behind and there's no place to pull over. Folks are driving in the breakdown lane."

"Turn around," I beg him. "Please?"

"Can't turn around neither," he says. "No room to maneuver. That little dog'll find you, son. Keep where you're at, he'll find us."

All around, horns are honking like mad, popping off at those crazy dogs in the big SUV, and we're lurching along at less than a mile an hour, bumper to bumper, so close you can't even open a car door, and I know in my heart why Bandy jumped out of the van. I can feel what he's feeling. He's running away from what frightens him, trying to get to a place that's safe. And now he's all alone in traffic, with a million cars on the highway and drivers who are frustrated and angry and frightened of what may happen to everything they've left behind. Drivers who won't be looking out for some little dog, that's for sure.

If he gets under those angry wheels they'll squish him like a bug.

I can't let it happen, can't let Bandy get run over. No way! So I wriggle out through the open window, inches from those awful snarling Dobermans. *Save my dog*, that's all that's in my brain.

Grammy starts wailing my name before my feet hit the pavement.

"I'm gonna get Bandy!" I shout back to her. "Don't worry! We'll catch up! I'll be right back, promise!"

I duck under the snarling Dobermans, feel their angry spit on my neck, and then I'm running low in the narrow gap between the moving cars, with everybody honking. A few vehicles behind the church van, a tinted window rolls down and a man in a straw cowboy hat says, "Fool! Leave the dog!" and makes to swipe his big hand at me — he's seen everything that's going on, obviously — but I duck away and he has to put his pickup truck in gear and go forward with the flow.

I squeeze around between the moving cars, slipping from bumper to bumper and finally make it over to the guardrail, hoping to catch sight of Bandy. I'm shouting, "Here boy! Bandit, come back!" but with all the cars and trucks and the big SUVs I can't see a little dog dodging between the tires, and maybe he can't hear me above all the horns and engine noises.

I'm so scared for Bandy that my heart feels like it might jump right out of my chest. What if I'm too late? What if he's already been run over? I keep ducking right and left, peering between the lines of traffic, all of it coming right at me, but I can't see him anywhere. We're on an elevated section of the highway, an on-ramp kind of deal, so he can't have run off to the side because there's nowhere to go. He can't really get away from all the cars and trucks, not here, not for a long way back, so he has to be somewhere on the highway. Where is he? Why can't I see him?

Then it starts to rain — a warm drizzly rain — and that makes it even harder to see. I'm starting to think he really has been run over and killed when I hear *hi-hi-hi*, that silly little bark, letting me know where he is. There! Bandy, sitting on his haunches by the side of traffic maybe fifty yards away, peering at me from around a tire. Sitting on his butt in the rain and barking at me *hi-hi-hi*. So of course I run along the guardrail, intending to scoop him up and tell him what a bad boy he is. Then we'll turn around and catch up with Grammy and the pastor in slow-moving traffic, no harm no foul.

Except that's not the way it happens.

What happens is this. Bandy waits until I'm almost to him, and then he turns and scampers alongside the guardrail, against all that traffic, like he intends to lead me away from all the scary cars and horns and he hopes I'm smart enough to follow.

Dumb enough is more like it. Because that's what I do. I follow the dog. In the rain. With a hurricane coming. Dumb and dumber, running back into the storm.

One good thing about the rain. Nobody can see I'm crying.

7.

When the Wind Screams

I follow that dog for miles in the warm rain, through the stink of overheated cars and smelly exhaust fumes. Bandy keeps waiting for me to catch up and whenever I get in range he scoots ahead, wagging his tail and yipping at me like he's trying to say something. Maybe apologizing, because he must sense how bad I feel, leaving Grammy behind probably worried sick about me, and there's nothing the pastor can do about it because he has to keep that van going forward in the pressing traffic without even a breakdown lane where he can pull over.

Truth is, I'm doing a really bad thing. I know it, too. Much as I love that stupid dog, jumping out of the van was flat wrong. No question. Chasing Bandy through the rain, alongside all those honking cars, every step I take is the wrong one. But I keep thinking I'll catch him and then go back and find the van and everything will be okay.

Until Bandy finally scampers down off the highway onto a regular street, into this empty wet neighborhood of saggy clapboard houses, some of them boarded up.

Then I know for sure where he's going.

"Bandy! We can't go back! Come here, boy!"

But he won't stop, no matter how much I plead and beg. He's trotting along and wagging his tail like this is all a fun game. And me? I'm following in my squishy Nikes, clothes soaked through to the skin.

Not many people are left in Grammy's neighborhood, but now and then I see a few old gumbies peering at me from behind the wet windows. Shaking their heads because that boy out in the rain, he must be crazy.

They've got a point. Anyone with wheels is headed out of the city, away from the hurricane, and I'm letting a little dog lead me in the opposite direction. Crazy and stupid, totally. But I keep trudging along, my voice so hoarse I can barely shout at the dog.

Not that it does any good anyway, shouting for him to come back. Bandy has his own idea that he thinks is right. It started with him running away from the scary dogs, but at some point he decided to take me home, as close to home as he knew. That was his mission and he did it, like he had me on some kind of invisible leash.

When I finally trudge up to the porch he's quivering with doggy joy, rolling on his back and showing his belly to let me know how happy he is that he led me home, and I followed.

At this point I'm so wet and miserable and scared of what my mother's going to say that I can't even be mad at him.

"Don't suppose you have a key?" I ask.

He barks, wagging his tail.

"Didn't think so."

Great. So now I have to break into my great-grandmother's house, which probably makes me a criminal. I certainly feel like one, eyeing the other houses on the block to see if anybody is watching.

Nobody home, or if they are, they're not showing themselves.

I try the windows, find one that's not locked, force it up, and shimmy inside, landing with a thump. Then I open the front door and let Bandy in. He's like a little sponge, shaking drops in all directions, and I'm not much better. I get a bunch of towels from the bathroom and try to dry us off, but the dog thinks this is a game, and somehow we both end up wetter than when we started.

"Bet you're hungry, hey boy?"

He barks as if to say yes. No surprise, he's always hungry.

"Your food's in the church van," I tell him. "Maybe we can find something in Grammy's cupboards."

There are cans on the shelves, mostly soups. Turns out Bandy likes beef stew. I have some myself, not bothering to heat it up. Tastes kind of weird that way, but I'm so hungry it doesn't matter.

After slurping up his food Bandy turns around in a little circle and instantly falls asleep with his head on my foot.

A gust of wind rattles the windows. Sends a shiver through me, even though it's still hot. Funny thing, I never expected to find the house so lonesome. The place was full of Miss Trissy and all her stories and her pictures and her songs, and for some reason me and Bandy don't seem to fill up the empty.

Thinking about it only makes me feel worse, so I slip my foot out from under the dog and go to that big old black telephone and make that dreaded call to my mom. I'm slotting the numbers in that rotary dial, heart pounding, afraid of what she'll say. From the moment I slipped out of the van I knew I'd have to make this call, but that doesn't make it easier.

She picks up on the first ring and goes, "Tell me you're okay!"

"I'm okay, Mom. We're at Grammy's. That's where Bandy ran to."

I explain how my cell phone is in my backpack and the backpack is in the church van, so I couldn't call until I got to Grammy's house. I tell her how sorry I am for what happened but it wasn't my fault, I had to do it.

Mom cuts me off and says, "We'll deal with that later. Your poor great-grandmother is in a state, of course. Pastor Daniels called the police from his vehicle to report a boy lost on the highway but obviously they didn't find you. With an entire city evacuating, the cops have their hands full, but as soon as we hang up I'm going to call them and wait on the line as long as it takes and give them your location. When they show up, young man, you will let them take you to a storm shelter. There will be no argument on this subject."

"What about Bandy? I heard on the radio the shelters don't allow pets."

"I said no argument."

She means it, so I shut up.

"I understand you love that little dog," she says, relenting.

"I thought he'd get run over!" I blurt.

Mom takes a deep breath and then goes, "I'm hanging up to call the police. Maybe there are shelters that allow pets. I'll call you back as soon as I find out."

"Okay, Mom."

"Love you."

"Love you, too."

Hours go by.

The cops never do show up, not that night.

Not ever, actually.

Hours tick by, one long minute at a time. Hours and hours, and the phone doesn't ring, and it doesn't ring, and it keeps not ringing.

Outside, in the dark, the wind begins to talk. Well, not talk, exactly. More like little noises shrieking up one side of the roof and down the other, like a pack of crazy invisible monsters coming through the night to get us.

There's nothing to do but curl up on the couch with Bandy and try to watch TV through the static and wait for the phone to ring. The only thing on Grammy's one station is the hurricane, the same stuff over and over, and eventually my eyelids get heavy and I must have fallen asleep, because the next thing I know the TV is off and the room is dark.

The whole house is dark.

Black dark, not even a glimmer of light.

The power is out.

Bandy whimpers, trying to curl closer. He's what woke me, licking my chin.

"Stay here, boy," I whisper.

Something about the darkness makes me want to whisper.

I feel my way along to the telephone table and lift the heavy receiver, hoping to hear Mom's voice on the other end, telling me not to worry.

But there's no one there. The phone line is dead and the wind . . . well, the wind begins to scream.

8.

Something Big and Bad

A gust slams into the side of the house, rattling the windows. Bandy hunkers down on his tummy, whimpering. Obviously scared of hurricanes. Smart dog.

The storm gets stronger and stronger, until the house whimpers, too.

"We'll be okay," I keep telling the dog. Hoping it's true.

Then a window explodes, punched in by a falling branch. The broken tree-fingers scratch at the windowsill like a thing alive and Bandy goes nuts, as if he thinks he can scare the storm away by barking at it.

I'm crouched in a doorway in the middle of the house, as far from the windows as possible. Knees to my chin, hands protecting my head because that's what Mom always said we should do in a tornado. *If the roof flies off, don't look up,* that was Mom's other instruction about a tornado. But this isn't a tornado dancing through a town, exploding buildings and then going away. Bad as a tornado might be (and it must be terrible), at least it doesn't last long — it wrecks the world and then moves on. But the hurricane feels like it's here to stay and getting stronger by the minute.

The wind, the wind, the wind. Please stop the wind.

That's what keeps running through my mind. Making bets with myself that the storm is about to weaken, that the wind will give up any second now, but I keep losing those bets and the storm keeps blowing.

Please, please stop.

Begging doesn't work. Praying doesn't work. Nothing stops the storm. It just keeps on howling and shaking the house.

Darkness melts into dawn and as the sky gets lighter the wind screams higher and higher.

Over the screaming wind a shrill, stuttering kind of noise comes from the street. Sounds almost like crazy laughter, rising and falling, falling and rising. Finally I can't stand it anymore and crawl over to the broken window to have a look. The crazy noise is coming from a stop sign at the corner of the street. The wind makes the sign quiver violently and bend almost to the ground, but the sign keeps popping back up, as if trying to shake off the great force of the hurricane.

That's sort of how I feel, like that stop sign, quivering inside but fighting back.

The noises the hurricane makes are like nothing I've ever heard before: the shriek of roof shingles exploding into the sky like flocks of frightened birds.

Metal screaming as if in pain.

Ripped-apart trees rising in a whirl, like ingredients in a giant blender.

The eerie *snap!* and *ping!* as phone lines and power lines break away from the poles, uncoiling against the wet ground like giant whips.

The hurricane keeps on coming. On and on it roars by like an insane train that never seems to end.

Bandy keeps licking at my hand. He thinks if he's a good-enough dog I'll make it stop.

I hug him closer.

Another window explodes. Spatters of rain hit us inside the house. Rain like hard, tiny bullets.

Please stop. Please stop. Please please please.

Here's the thing about being afraid: after a while it makes you tired. As the hours go by I start to nod off, chin lolling on my chest. It feels like the hurricane has always been here and always will be, so I might as well sleep. The storm invades my dreams and I see my mom with her yellow hair streaming in the wind, yelling words I can't make out. Miss Trissy is there, too, trying to sing louder than the wind, but she can't and rain comes from her eyes, soaking me to the skin.

When I wake up the storm has softened. The wind is still blowing, rattling the world, but the air feels lighter. There's a patch of blue in the morning sky and for just a moment, no more than a heartbeat, I'm convinced the hurricane was a bad dream. But the branch sticking through the broken window is real, and so is the fact that rain reached deep inside the house, dampening my clothes.

The damp doesn't matter. We survived, me and Bandy. The worst of the storm is over and the roof is still on the house. Broken windows can be fixed. There's a funny bubble deep in my chest, like a balloon expanding. Joy. I'm so happy to be alive. So happy we both survived.

"Come on, Bandy, let's see what it looks like out there."

Bandy's still fearful, but he follows me out to the front porch. The wind is coming from the other side of the house and we're sort of protected from the worst of it. There are leaves and broken branches everywhere, and strange things left by the storm. A pair of new sneakers with the laces still tied together. A plastic bottle filled with milk. A Scooby-Doo pajama top tied in knots. A pink rubber ball. And a little brown bird with a broken neck.

Poor little thing, I'm thinking, *poor dead bird*.

Bandy barks sharply, as if he senses something off in the distance, and a moment later there's a deep booming noise, like the sound when you thump the side of an empty fuel oil tank, only deeper. Deep enough to feel it rumble through your bones and in the bottom of your belly.

Not a good noise. Something big and bad just happened. Next I hear a *pop-pop-pop*, like corks released from a row of bottles, and the fat, wet noise of rushing water.

That's when I see it with my own eyes. A manhole cover pops into the air, releasing a geyser of brown water. Then another and another, right down the street, one, two, three, four. Torrents of water surge up from the ground, and more of it pours in from all sides, spilling around and under the houses, carrying debris along in the wake.

Enough water to fill the world.

9.

Trapped

Bandy tugs at my pant leg, frantic to drag me back inside.

Knees shaking, I slam the door and turn the lock, as if that will keep the water out. And it does — for about ten seconds. Then the rising flood gushes through the gap under the door. The pressure of it throbs against the door panels like something alive.

Water squirts through the keyhole and around my fingers. And a whole lot more water gushes over the sill of the broken window, like some huge faucet that can't be turned off.

Think! Rising water, what am I supposed to do? What did Grammy say?

Rising water drove us up into the attic. She'd pointed at a square panel in the ceiling. *Imagine me climbing through that little hole in the ceiling? Well, I did!*

There must be a ladder. But where is it? There's no room for a ladder in the cupboard where Grammy keeps her canned goods. Maybe she got rid of the ladder because she can't climb it anymore. Or maybe it broke. Or maybe she keeps the ladder outside in the yard, in which case it's already floating away.

Ladder or no ladder I have to do something. The water is almost up to my knees, which makes it harder to move. Heart slamming, I slog through the flood, fighting my way into the kitchen. Bandy, splashing ahead of me, leaps onto the kitchen table and wags his tail, like he discovered something important — and maybe he has.

"Good idea, boy."

I grab the rickety table and drag it into the hallway, under the opening to the attic. Shaking like a leaf, I climb onto the table. Standing on my toes with arms stretched high, I'm able to push up the panel that covers the attic opening. I shove it to one side.

It's black up there, and boiling hot. Steaming air pours from the attic down into the hallway. Even standing on the table, the opening is still too high for me to climb up and inside. Can't quite get a grip.

"Bandy! Wait here, okay? Good dog!"

I leave him on the table, looking puzzled, while I slog back into the kitchen and grab a wooden chair that's already starting to float away.

Water is up to my thighs and still rising. Almost but not quite high enough to make the table float.

I have to do this quickly or it will be too late.

Don't panic, I tell myself, *just do it.*

Not so easy when water is pouring in the windows and under the doors and streaming through every crack in the old house. Pushing hard, I slog back to the hallway and prop the chair on top of the table.

Bandy instantly leaps into the chair, getting as far from the rising water as possible.

"Smart boy," I tell him. "You first."

I climb onto the wobbly table and grab him up in my arms and for once he doesn't squirm. Balancing on the tippy chair, I boost Bandy the Wonder Dog up into the attic. With the added height of the chair under my feet I'm able to poke my head and shoulders into the attic. It isn't, as I'd thought, totally dark up there. A little daylight comes through a vent on one end of the building, making me slightly less afraid. Not that I'm really scared of the dark — the night-light in my bedroom went away at least a year ago — but there's something about total, black darkness that makes my stomach clench.

Bandy, paws skittering on the rafters around the opening, desperately licks my face, urging me to join him.

That's my plan. But now is when I wish I'd put more effort into gym class. Mr. Carmody the gym teacher made us hang on a bar and see how many chin-ups we could do. I could barely do one. So I made some joke that the whole thing was lame and refused to try it again. Mr. Carmody, he shrugged and said, "It's up to you, Zane. I can't make you stronger, but you can, if you put a little effort into it."

I never did "put a little effort into it." What was the point? To be ready in case a flood chases you into your great-grandmother's attic in New Orleans? No way. Stuff like that never happens — except it did! And now I have to do a chin-up because my life depends on it. No choice but to grab hold of a rafter and pull myself into the attic, to escape from the rising water.

Go on, do it. Now or never. Chin-up or drown, your choice.

My whole body is shaking — a kind of heart-slamming weakness that makes it hard to stand up without my knees knocking, let alone hoist myself into the attic. But on the very first try I pull myself through the opening, no problem. I lie there in the attic sweating like a pig, with the rafters poking me in the back and Bandy happily licking my face.

Amazing. Apparently being afraid to die makes you strong — or at least able to do one very important chin-up.

My eyes gradually adjust to the dimness. The attic is hot as an oven and really small. In the center, where the roof peaks, there's barely enough room for me to turn over and crawl. Except for a few boards near the center of the attic there's no floor over the rafters. Slip and your knee will go straight through the ceiling, just like in the cartoons.

Bandy barks at the opening. I peek over the edge into the hallway below and see something so amazing and so awful that despite the terrible heat, a chill goes through me.

The water is still swirling into the house, still rising. Another few feet and it will pour up into the attic.

We're trapped, me and Bandy. Trapped in the attic with no way to get out. Then I remember something Grammy said when she was telling the story about escaping the flood.

Henry brung him a little hatchet in case we had to chop through the roof.

Too bad I didn't think of that. Not that I'd ever seen a hatchet around the house. But what if they left it up in the attic for the next storm? What if the hatchet has been laying in the dark all those years, waiting for me to find it?

I scramble over the rafters, searching for the hatchet.

10.

A Face in the Window

Crawling over rafters on my belly, I run my fingertips into every dark corner of the attic, willing the hatchet to be there. Wanting it so much I can almost feel the weight of the handle, the heft of the blade.

Wanting doesn't make it so. My desperate fingers find only dust and splinters.

Meanwhile, underneath us, the house shifts like a weary old wrestler fighting to stay in one place, timbers moaning as the water presses from all sides. Every now and then something heavy bumps into the side of the house and everything shudders.

I'm worried the old building will twist off the foundation and tip over, drowning us for sure. But the house doesn't tip over. And despite the gurgling splashes from below, the water hasn't come up into the attic. Not quite. It gets within a foot of the opening, close enough to reach out and touch. And then it pauses, as if deciding whether or not to swallow us in one big gulp.

Don't know how long I'm lying there staring at the water level, but it feels like hours. Long enough to think about all the things I've done wrong lately. Flying down to Smellyville in the first place — that was a mistake right there. Only if I never came down I'd never have met my great-grandmother or heard her stories about the old days, or seen the pictures of my father when he was my age. Him and his little brother that ran around with bath towels for capes, pretending to be Superman. And hearing Grammy sing like an angel, that was pretty cool. Her fussing over me and everything. But where did it get me, all that stupid family stuff? Trapped in an attic, that's where! And then of course the stupidest mistake off all, letting Bandy jump out of the van window. I should have been holding him tight. Dogs jump out of cars all the time, I knew that. What was I thinking? And leaving Grammy stuck in evacuation traffic without even saying good-bye, that was a really terrible thing to do. So terrible I can't stand to think about it, but there's no way to stop my brain from going over it again and again, every mistake, every stupid thing I've ever done or said. My brain won't shut up, it keeps going, *Zane Dupree you are a fool, you are the dumbest human being on Planet Earth. You left your cell phone in the van and ran away to save your stupid dog and you can't even save your own stupid self. What were you thinking? Now look what you've done, crawled up into an attic to die like some drowned rat. You haven't got so much as a candy bar in your pocket and no water to drink and it must be a hundred degrees and getting hotter.*

The floodwater smells like when the toilet backs up, only worse.

Way worse.

I'm surrounded by filthy brown water and nothing to drink. *Nice going you moron, you crud bucket, you dumb-butt dipstick doodlebrain.* What's that rhyme my mom used to read me? *Water water everywhere nor any drop to drink?* Something about being on a boat in the middle of the ocean and running out of drinking water. That's sort of how the attic feels, like me and Bandy are shipwrecked on an ocean so hot the water is almost boiling. Like all the hottest days of the hottest summers have combined in that little attic.

Sweat drips from the end of my nose, from my chin, from my scalp and hair, from my eyes.

Hot, hot, hot. Unbearably, unbelievably hot.

Bandy is panting so hard I'm afraid he might die of the heat. Did you know dogs can't sweat? The only way they have to keep cool is panting, and it doesn't work as well as sweating. I know because somebody left a dog in a car at the mall last year, when it got to be a hundred degrees in the parking lot, and the poor dog died. So it can happen, I'm not making it up.

Finally I get sick of waiting for the smelly water to go down — it hasn't budged an inch either way — and decide to crawl over to the little vent at the end of the attic. Slants of sunlight streak through the vent, but maybe it'll be cooler over there, that's what I'm hoping, and at least Bandy can pant fresher air.

"Hey, Bandy, follow me," I urge him, my voice hoarse.

Bandy doesn't want to move. That's when I really start to worry he might die if I don't do something to help.

Taking the dog in my arms I wriggle along the rafters on my back. The poor little guy is so overheated he can barely whimper, but seems to understand that I'm trying to help him.

Peering through the slits of the vent I can see, what else, lots and lots of water. Water water everywhere, and all of it hot and stinky and disgusting. Sun glinting off the water feels like a hot nail pressing into my forehead, but the air near the vent is slightly cooler. Or maybe that's my imagination, hard to tell.

"Hey, Bandy? Feeling any better? Keep panting, boy. It's good for you."

My mouth is so dry I can hardly talk, but Bandy understands and squirms closer to the vent. There's a little air moving through the slats, but not enough to make much of a difference. Bandy watches me through one heavily lidded eye, like he can barely stay awake. He's not even bothering to pant very much.

That can't be good.

"Hey, boy. Stay awake, okay? Keep me company. That's your job, right?"

Exhausted by the heat, Bandy stops panting and closes his eyes.

Do something! I urge myself.

The idea that Bandy might not survive makes me scared and furious at the same time. I try yanking at the wooden slats, but my sweaty hands keep slipping away. I'm so mad and frustrated I want to cry. Not that it would make any difference, because my eyes are so full of salty sweat that it's hard to see.

My mom is always saying don't be mad, be smart.

Think. What's the strongest part of the human body? Legs, Zane, legs. You know that. Use your brain. And your feet.

I swivel around on the boards and gather as much strength as I've got left. Then I kick the vent slats with both feet, hard as I can.

The slats crack.

I never knew breaking wood could sound so good.

Three more kicks and all the slats are cleared from the vent.

Right away I can feel slightly cooler air flowing into the attic. I position Bandy so his head is sticking out of the open vent and he perks up a little, his pink tongue hanging down. They say dogs don't smile, but I swear that little dog is smiling at me.

In a few minutes he's even got enough strength to bark.

After all the flooding, the water has become perfectly still, like a dirty mirror. In the reflection me and Bandy are looking down from the open vent to the surface of the water just below. Has it gone down at all? Maybe. Or is that wishful thinking?

Bandy barks again.

What's he barking at? From this angle the only things clearly visible are the peaks of other roofs sticking above the water and floating branches and hunks of junk that might be parts of ripped-apart houses, and the terrible hot reflection of the sun, burning like a blazing white fire in the water. And far away, in silhouette against the sunlight, something gliding by.

Might be a boat.

Might be people in the boat, one big, one small.

It's there for a moment, way out beyond the roofs, and then gone, swallowed up by the blazing sun.

I try to shout, but my throat is so dry and raw that nothing much comes out. I croak a pathetic little "*help help*" that sounds more like a whisper than a shout.

No one could hear me, certainly not that far away. But Bandy keeps barking, regular as clockwork, and finally I get so tired of trying to shout, trying to make my voice work, that I fall asleep — or maybe I pass out.

In my dream I'm back in my own room in New Hampshire and the air feels like molten syrup. Syrup so hot and heavy that I can't move. My mom is in the next room, but she can't hear me because the shout is deep inside me and it won't come out. I try panting like a dog but that doesn't work because my tongue is so dry it feels as crispy as a slice of fried bacon.

Somewhere far, far away a dog is barking.

"Yo, boy! Hey! Wake up!"

My eyelids are sticky, but I manage to crack them open. There in the opening, holding the edges of the vent with both hands, is a skinny black girl with big dark eyes and wild hair.

11.

The Big Whoops

The girl with the wild hair says, "Hey, you stupid or what? Wasn't for this little dog nobody know you in there."

I try to answer back, but the words get stuck in my throat.

Another voice, much deeper, goes, "Don't mind Malvina. She a little wasp that keep on stingin'."

My eyes slowly come into sharper focus. A battered green canoe floats in the water just below the vent opening. In one end, waving her thin arms, is the girl with the big eyes and the wild hair. About my age but smaller than me, and wicked skinny. In the other end, keeping balance with a paddle, sits a calm-looking, light-skinned black man with clunky, black-framed eyeglasses and scrawny dreads poking out from under a straw top hat. Like a Mad Hatter kind of hat, the kind with a curvy brim. There's a pink feather in the hatband, sticking up like an exclamation point.

"It was Malvina heard the dog," the man explains in a rumbly, musical voice. "The child got ears like a bat."

"I ain't no bat!" she protests, folding her arms across her skinny chest.

"All it mean, dawlin', you got good ears," he explains. "Bat can hear a pin drop."

"Ain't no dawlin', neither!"

He smiles and shakes his head as if to say, *see what I have to put up with?* but in a way that makes me think he doesn't mind. "Best get you down," he suggests, paddling the canoe alongside the building. "Must be hot enough in there to boil yo brain."

Getting into the canoe proves to be difficult. I back out through the vent with my legs kicking air. Bandy barks and whines and licks at my hands like he's worried he'll be left behind. Strong hands grab hold of my feet and guide me down as the deep voice of the man in the funny hat tells me to keep calm, that I'm doing fine.

"There now. You good."

All of a sudden I'm crouched in the middle of the tippy canoe, holding on for dear life.

The skinny girl, Malvina, she's grinning at me, showing the gap in her teeth. "Don't fall in," she teases, full of mischief. "The water got snakes."

"Snakes?"

She nods happily, as if snakes in the water is her idea of a good time.

"Don't worry about no snakes," says the man in the funny hat. "All you gotta do, stay in the boat."

"Ain't a boat," Malvina insists. "This a canoe."

The man shrugs and says, "The young lady happy to point out any mistake."

Bandy is barking like mad, wanting to follow me into the canoe. The thing is, now that I'm sitting down and holding on to the sides, I'm worried that reaching for the dog will tip us over. And the idea of snakes, even snakes I can't see, has me spooked.

The man in the hat seems to understand and goes, "Let me think what we can do."

He's trying to maneuver the canoe alongside the edge of the roof when all of a sudden Bandy gives a mighty yelp of frustration and launches himself through the air.

The little dog hits me square in the chest. I catch him and then we're tipping over. Me and Bandy and the girl and the man with the hat, we all splash backward into the water as the canoe slips out from under us.

Bandy, totally freaked, climbs onto my head, pushing me under, into that dark, snaky water.

When I come back up, coughing and spitting, I'm more scared than the dog. Because I can't see the girl. And all that shows of the man with the rumbly voice is the funny top hat with the pink feather, bobbing in the water like a toy.

12.

Terrible Things

Later, when I'd had time to think about it, the thing that impressed me most about the man with the hat was how he kept so calm. I was all frantic, convinced I'd drowned two people, but by the time my eyes cleared he'd already lifted the girl up to the roof and was reaching out a hand to help me.

"No big thang," he says, shaking water from his dreads. "We gots a little wet is all."

Like it happens every day, being tipped out of a canoe. And the weird thing is, the cause of it all, my stupid dog Bandy, he's balanced on the peak of the roof with his tail wagging. Shook the water off and doesn't even look wet. It's only us dumb humans that are soaked to the skin.

"I'm sorry," I say, spitting out dirty water. "Really really sorry."

The man has got hold of the swamped canoe and pulls it under the eave. "Accidents happen," he says. "No apology required. Okay, next thing I'm fixin' to get my hat and then bail out our transportation. You children keep hold this roof till I'm done. We good?"

He's looking firm at the girl.

"Good," she says with a nod.

He scoops up his straw top hat, takes the feather from the brim and holds it in his teeth, and uses the hat to bail out the canoe. When he's done he slips the feather back in the brim band, puts the hat on top of his head, and shows us how to slide down the roof into the canoe while he holds it steady.

When we're safe in the canoe, the girl in the front and me in the middle holding Bandy, the man hoists himself into the stern of the canoe, making it look easy. After he's settled he opens the latch of a little storage compartment, takes out a plastic bottle of water, and hands it to me.

"Sip at it slow," he suggests. "Maybe po' a little in yo hand, let that dog lick it up."

Warm water never tasted so good. I nod thank you and Bandy makes a grateful whimper.

"There now, we good to go," the man says, straightening the clunky, black-framed eyeglasses on his slightly bent nose. "Keep a sharp lookout for my paddle. Can't have drifted too far."

That's another thing for me to feel sorry about, that the paddle got lost when we tipped over, but before I can really get to worrying about it the girl shouts, "Yo! Over there!"

The man dips his hands and arms into the water, like he's swimming the canoe along, and slowly strokes over to where she's pointing. Sure enough he finds the paddle, barely visible in the dark water.

"Just like Christmas mornin'," he says, picking it up. "Okay, we back on mission. Next stop, someplace dry."

"Where we goin', Tru?" the girl asks.

"Place I know." Then he turns to me and says, "I'm Trudell Manning. Some folks call me Tru. Miss Malvina Rawlins you already know. Me and Malvina, we family, most. Not blood, but family just the same."

"You my blood, Tru!" Malvina pipes up.

"Whatever you say, dawlin'."

Then he looks at me patiently, as if waiting for me to respond.

"Oh, yeah. Sorry. I'm Zane Dupree."

"Dupree? That a local name, but you ain't."

"No, sir, I'm not from around here."

"Makes no difference," he says with a shrug. "You one of us now."

He dips the paddle and the canoe begins to move along, gathering speed. We glide away from what's left of Grammy's house and into another world, or so it seems. A world of rooftops poking above the flood like little black islands, and trees clawing up through the water like the gnarled hands of the drowned. A world where the water and the sky melt together, until you can't tell where one begins and the other ends.

The air feels wet and heavy and stinks of sewer and oil and smoke. Somewhere, something is burning, but we can't see what, only the smoke like a gray smear in the sky.

We glide along for a while and then the skinny girl, Malvina Rawlins, she turns to me and announces, out of the blue, "Tru a famous musician."

"Oh yeah? Cool."

"He play trumpet, cornet, tuba, trombone," Malvina says, ticking the instruments off on her fingers. "Anything brass, Tru play it real good."

"Not trombone," he says, chuckling.

"I heard you!" she exclaims.

He pauses to rest his paddle. "For your amusement, dawlin'. But the fact is, I'm not a slide man. Trumpet, cornet, pocket trumpet, yes. Tuba in a pinch. But not trombone. Not really."

"Could if you wanted!" she says, expression triumphant.

He seems pleased by the notion. "No doubt."

"Tru jammin' with all the big names," she says proudly. "He down with Wynton, Kermit, Junior. Everybody!"

Mr. Tru smiles indulgently. "Studio work," he explains to me. "Wynton Marsalis, Kermit Ruffins, Harry Connick, Jr., Randy Newman, the Neville Brothers. Anybody needs a horn, I'm there. But backing up famous musicians don't make me famous. Wish it did."

"You famous to me!" Malvina insists.

He grins, dips the paddle into the filthy water, and says he doesn't know how far we'll have to go, exactly. "Flood change everything," he explains, glancing around at the landscape of submerged buildings. "We got to feel our way along till we get to a place I recognize."

"So we lost?" Malvina asks, teasing.

"Naw, naw," he says. "We not lost. No suh. Got a compass in my head always points me right."

"True dat," says Malvina, nodding.

He notices my confusion and explains. " 'True dat' has nothing to do with my name. It's the way we say 'that's true,' only it means something more. Something like 'I agree with you because we both see things the same way.' Nowadays it kind of a cliché thang 'cause everybody say it, even tourist."

Malvina giggles. "True dat, Tru!" she says.

"Now she playin' with us," he says, grinning.

We keep going, Mr. Tru paddling in a steady rhythm, gliding us along. After a while I get to staring down at my hands, thinking about my mom and Grammy and how I really messed up this time. Bandy snuggles closer but for some reason that doesn't make me feel any better. Feeling sorry for myself and not really paying attention to where we're going until Mr. Tru says, in a voice of wonder, "Will you look at that."

We've come out from among the sunk houses and into an open area, big as a lake. And right in the middle is this giant, rusty red steel box, a great huge thing as long as a city block. Looks like it dropped out of the sky and crushed a bunch of houses that stick out from under it like water-soaked kindling.

Impossible, but there it is.

"That a barge from the Industrial Canal," he says softly. "Musta busted through the levee, knocked all them homes off their foundations."

He turns away, as if it is much too painful to see such a thing.

After that I really start paying attention. All kinds of stuff floats by as we glide through the water. A basketball. An empty Styrofoam cooler. Soda bottles, hunks of wood. Plastic toys, cups and bowls. A big old rusty water heater. A red gasoline jug. Parts of a doll. Papers, books, clothing. Precious things and garbage all mixed together, lifted by the flood.

We keep going for a while, nobody saying much, like what we're seeing is beyond words. Things still have names but they're different in the water, out of place, and don't look right. At one point we come upon a long skinny wooden thing that seems strangely familiar. Takes me a moment to figure out what it is: the little wind-vane steeple from the New Mission Zion Baptist Church, floating sideways. A big crow with black glittering eyes perches on the fat end of the steeple, squawking as we glide by.

Despite the muggy heat, I shiver deep in my bones.

Everything looks so strange and wrong and mixed up. Like a bad dream, except that even in my worst nightmare I could never have imagined, say, a huge mass of bugs swarming over the surface of the water, splashing and twirling around like crazy things all knotted together.

"Cockroaches," Mr. Tru says, steering away from the swarm of insane insects.

"You 'fraid of bugs?" Malvina asks me.

"If they bite," I admit.

"Roach don't bite, do it, Tru?"

"Not normal, no," he says. "Can't say what a creature might do, flooded out of home."

We pass another swarm of roaches. No snakes, though. I hope they're kidding about snakes in the water, but just to be sure I keep my hands inside the boat. Bandy has settled into my lap like it's no big deal riding in a canoe through a flooded city with crazy birds and clicking bugs and a giant house-crushing barge and a group of garbage bags slowly bobbing in the current.

Something's wrong about the garbage bags. I don't know what, exactly, not right away.

"Terrible thing happened here," Mr. Tru says softly. "We gone steer our way through it all, don't let nothing touch us."

He paddles strong and fast, veering left.

"Don't look back," he advises. "Nothing we can do."

Malvina starts to sing "Jesus Loves Me" in a high, clear voice, and that's when I know that what I'm seeing isn't garbage bags. It's the barely floating remains of those who couldn't get away, who were too old or sick to climb up into the attic like me and Bandy did.

Dead people, drowned by the flood.

Malvina begins to weep and can't finish the hymn. Bandy crawls out of my lap and goes to her and she hugs him to her chest. "Good dog," she says, sniffing back her tears. "Good dog."

13.

When It Can't Get Worse

The light is fading from the dreary sky when Mr. Tru finally rests his paddle and announces, "We here."

The canoe nudges up against a flight of stairs that rises out of the oily dark water. The ground floor of the building remains submerged but the second-floor apartment is, as he promised, above the flood. The apartment, he explains, belongs to a friend.

"Della won't mind," he says, leaving the canoe lashed to a railing. "She in Natchez with her daughter."

But the door is locked.

"Course it is," he says softly, and turns to Malvina. "Can you climb in through that little window, dawlin'?"

She squints at the small window. "No problem!" and in less than a minute she's opening the front door with a mischievous grin. "There's a big TV an' a AC!" she announces as we step inside.

A big TV and a new air conditioner, but no electricity. Not a surprise, really, since most of the power lines have been blown down or carried away by the flood. Mr. Tru says we'll have to make do.

"Della keep a nice kitchen," he says. "We ain't gonna starve."

"Is there a phone I can use?" I ask. "Sometimes a landline phone will work even when the power's out."

"Everything down," he says, shaking his head. "Ain't got my cell but even if I did, I doubt it work. Day after a bad storm the phones always out and this weren't no regular hurricane. Tomorrow we find us some dry ground, wherever it at, and get you back with your family."

Bandy is sniffing every corner of the small apartment, including under the couch and the bed, and keeps making little happy yelps like he's discovered something interesting.

"Did the owner have a cat?" I ask.

"Queenie," Mr. Tru says, surprised. "But Della never leave that cat behind. No way."

Doesn't matter that the cat is gone, Bandy can still smell it everywhere. He's wagging his tail and looking for a friend because Bandy is one of those weird dogs who likes cats and wants to play. But he comes running fast enough when I locate a can of cat food and pop the lid.

Turns out a hungry dog will eat cat food, no problem. And humans will eat canned spaghetti, no problem there, either. Me and Mr. Tru share a can of spaghetti and some stale bread while Malvina has a bowl of cereal and the last of the milk in the refrigerator.

"You children drink up what's left," he suggests. "'Nother hour or two, everything in that fridge start to go bad."

Malvina pours the rest of the milk into a glass and offers it to me. I shake my head. She eagerly drains the glass and wipes her mouth with a paper napkin. "My mom always say don't leave nothing in the glass."

"So where's your mom?" I ask, thinking of my own mother.

Malvina stares down at the table and frowns. "In a hospital," she says.

"Oh," I say. "What's wrong with her?"

"Did I say there was something wrong with my momma? Did I? Don't you be sayin' there is."

"Sorry."

"Don't you be sorry! Don't need no sorry from no stupid boy!"

She glares at me so hard it makes my face hot.

Mr. Tru takes off his hat and places it carefully on the kitchen chair beside him. Without the jaunty hat he looks older. His dreads are a little thin and have some gray in them, although it's hard to see in the fading light. And when he removes his black-framed glasses to wipe the sweat from his brow, his eyes are puffy and the whites are kind of yellow.

"Malvina's mother left her in my care," he explains. "It a temporary kind of situation and I am happy to oblige."

"Where's *your* mom, huh?" Malvina says, her chin jutting out. "How come she ain't here?"

So I explain about visiting my great-grandmother and how our flight got canceled and how I jumped out of the church van to look for Bandy and all.

Mr. Tru nods along with my story.

"Beatrice Jackson that sing in the choir? Miss Trissy? That was her place we found you at? Oh my. That woman a legend in the neighborhood! Drop so much as a cigarette butt on her street and you in trouble. She still go 'mmm, mmm' all the time?"

I nod.

"So," he says, super casual, "what your daddy's name?"

"Gerald."

"Uh-huh. You say he passed?"

"Before I was born. You knew him?"

He hesitates and says, "Knew of him, you might say. Not personal."

I like it that he doesn't make a fuss about my father being dead, even if he does know something he doesn't care to share. Fine by me. I mean, what does it matter? My father and his got-hissef-killed brother are ancient history, okay? Water under the bridge, or over it, or whatever.

Except it turns out Mr. Tru is not quite finished with the subject.

"Comes to me that both of you have that in common, that your daddies passed before you was born," he says, folding his arms and looking from me to Malvina.

She doesn't react, not giving anything away. Then I shrug and she shrugs back, like we've both heard all we can stand about absent fathers, and there's no need for further conversation. She holds that blank, you-can't-touch-me expression for a while and then goes, "Why you talk so funny, huh?"

"Don't be rude, dawlin'," Mr. Tru says in a warning tone.

"It's okay," I say. "In New Hampshire we think *you* talk funny."

Malvina grins and shakes her head, like she approves that I came right back at her. "Everybody talk funny, I guess," she concedes. "So what they do in New Hampshire?"

"What they do everywhere else, I guess. The usual stuff."

"Like what?"

I shrug. "Nothing special. The grown-ups go to work, mostly, and the kids go to school and like that."

"And when you not in school?"

"We, um, play video games and hang at the mall or whatever."

It sounds so lame but I really miss it.

"Uh-huh. They do procession in New Hampshire?" Malvina asks.

When Mr. Tru sees me looking puzzled, he explains about funeral processions, which in New Orleans are a kind of solemn celebration. The city is famous for them. "Some tourists call it a jazz funeral. We make a parade through the neighborhood, so folks can pay respect to the one that passed. But with music. Everything in this city about the music."

"And dancing in the second line!" Malvina adds.

"Oh yeah, that, too. See, the first in line is the family and friends of the deceased, and the line that follows after the band is everybody else. We call it the 'second line.'"

Malvina says, eagerly, "Second line dress up and do this special step-walk dance you only do for funerals. And all the fine ladies dab their eyes with lace handkerchiefs and twirl their umbrellas, everything to the beat of a drum. Slow kind of beat, real mournful, all the way to the cemetery. Whole neighborhood come out to watch. You know somebody special passed if Tru blowin' his trumpet! On the way back from the cemetery he play 'Saints' and everybody dance, might be you don't even got to know the deceased but you dancin' 'cause Trudell Manning be playin' his high sweet music."

Sounds pretty weird to me, dancing at a funeral. I've only ever been to one funeral, when my mom's cousin died, and believe me nobody thought of dancing. They had these nasty little sandwiches they passed around on plates, and some people told stupid but kind of funny stories, and the only music was this dreary organ at the church and a couple of creaky hymns. Nobody danced, not even close.

"Be lot of funerals," Malvina points out. "Them that drowned."

"Never mind none of that now." Mr. Tru turns to me as he changes the subject. "So, how you get up that little attic?"

After I describe what happened, the water chasing me and Bandy inside, and how we climbed up on the table and chair,

Mr. Tru tells how the flood caught him by surprise, too. How he and Malvina just barely made it out of his home and into a canoe he had stored behind the house.

"House went under but my little fishin' canoe, it pop up just in time," he says. "Floodwaters come so fast it was all I could do to grab Malvina and get out. Left everything behind, including my phone and wallet and all my brass." He shudders a little at the recollection. "What happen, I fell asleep with my hat on. See, I stayed up all night, listening to that hurricane wind, and when it finally stopped howling I must have relaxed and nodded off, there in my best chair. Thought we'd come through it safe and sound, you understand? Next thing, my feet are getting wet."

Malvina chimes in. "I was sleeping. Thought it was a dream. Like me and my mom was at the pool and she was teaching me to swim."

I make sure not to ask nothing more about her mom and Mr. Tru gives me a little nod, like he approves of me keeping my mouth shut on that particular subject.

"Gone be dark soon," he announces, standing up from the table. "Malvina, dawlin', maybe you can find where Della keep her candles. Me and Zane take care of the canoe."

While she hunts eagerly through the cupboards, me and Bandy help him drag the canoe up the steps and into the apartment, where it suddenly looks much bigger than it did outside.

"Better safe than sorry," he says, satisfied. "No matter what else happen, we got our transportation."

Which makes me wonder, what does he mean? We've been blown down by a hurricane, flooded over our heads, lost our homes and everything in them, been baked by the heat and nearly drowned in the filthy water, paddled through swarms of flying cockroaches, seen houses crushed by a giant ship, and steered away from the terrible sight of floating bodies.

I'm thinking it can't get any worse. Until night comes, and the guns start firing.

14.

In the Dark of the World

Malvina?" Mr. Tru says. "Blow out that candle."

We sit in the dark and wait until the next gunshot makes us jump.

"Sound like some distance away," he says softly. "Likely young men showin' off, or lettin' folks know they there. Nothin' to worry us none. But no reason to advertise, so we keep the candle out."

After a while the shooting stops and things get quiet.

I creep up to a window to have a look outside. Only thing I can make out is something burning in the distance, orange flames roiling like a thing alive. Doesn't seem right that a house half-submerged in water can burn, but burn it does, and nobody to stop it.

"No fire department," Mr. Tru points out. "No police."

"How come?" I ask. "Where is everybody?"

He shrugs. "They 'vacuated with the rest, or don't care to enter this particular neighborhood, or ain't got here yet, or maybe all three. Whatever the reason, we on our own and that's the troot. Nobody look out for us but us."

"You look out for us, Tru," says Malvina, who hasn't moved from the kitchen table.

He nods, very serious. "Do my best," he says.

We sit in the heat of the night, the three of us, watching the fire light up the dark horizon. The house burns like a flaming wooden match dipped into a glass of oily black water. When at last the fire goes out, the dark of the world comes upon us. There are no stars in the sky, none that I can see. No streetlights or house lights. Nothing but black night and the faint sound of the flood lapping at the steps like it wants to come in.

Bandy has hunkered down in my lap. He whines a little now and then but mostly he's being good, as if he understands that he shouldn't make trouble at a time like this.

"Long day," Mr. Tru says. "Best rest while we got the chance."

Malvina won't go up on the bed near the window because she's afraid of the gunshots, so we drag the mattress to the closet floor. She crawls onto it, one skinny arm curled over her head, and falls asleep almost at once.

We leave the bedroom door open — she insisted on that — and retreat quietly into the living room. Mr. Tru settles into a big stuffed chair, stretching out his legs. "I might sit up for a spell," he says, glancing at the door. "You take the sofa."

"We could take turns," I offer. "You stand watch, then I'll relieve you, like they do in the army."

He chuckles. "No need," he says. "Get you some rest."

Bandy curls next to me on the sofa.

"Good boy," I whisper, scratching his ears. "We're gonna be okay. We're gonna be just fine."

Feels good saying so, but I'm not sure I believe it.

Bandy drops off, running in his sleep. I'm exhausted but can't sleep, no way, not with the air so hot and muggy, and all the thoughts racing through my head like crazy pinballs. Me and Grammy and the pastor and the hurricane and Mom on the phone, sounding so far away, and me following this little dog that keeps disappearing underneath cars, and my father and his brother flying like Superman, and dark clouds chasing our canoe, clouds we can't get away from, clouds that want to swallow us up, clouds with gunshots inside them, popping like sparks of lightning.

I wake up with Bandy licking my face and the faint light of dawn slanting through the curtains.

15.

Snake City

After breakfast — saltine crackers and peanut butter — we load some bottled water and canned goods into the canoe.

"Where we go if everything underwater?" Malvina wants to know. "Maybe we should stay, wait on your friend."

"Ain't a safe place round here," Mr. Tru says, looking warily out at where guns were shooting last night. "We got to find us some dry ground. Leastways get us to a workin' phone. Then maybe I try call my cousin Belinda, she got a place over to Algiers, might be it was above the flood. Might be."

"Might be," Malvina says, making a face. "Huh."

Mr. Tru gives her a look. "This a might-be world we livin' in, dawlin'. That just the way it be."

"Sorry," says Malvina, looking apologetic. "You right, Tru. Naw, I mean to say you *might* be right."

Then she gives him a big, triumphant grin.

He snorts and shakes his head. "I ain't never win with you, dawlin'. I got the music, but you got the words, no doubt."

I'm not sure what they're talking about exactly, but they both seem pleased with each other, and an hour after dawn we paddle into the thin daylight, into the muggy heat, knowing it will get hotter as the sun rises. Flood level looks about the same, with one-story houses showing only their roofs above the water. The water itself glistens, filthy and clotted with the things it has carried away. Crows complain from the crooks of half-drowned trees. Small white seagulls swoop just above the water, fighting over scraps. Out at the blurry edge, where the sky meets the water, smoke rises in black billows, as if the water itself is burning.

Suddenly a hot breeze wrinkles the floodwaters, followed by the rush of an orange helicopter charging sideways through the sky. "Coast Guard!" Mr. Tru shouts in approval. "Somebody finally show up!"

The helicopters become a familiar noise. Can't always see them but we can hear them coming and going all day long, chugging across the sky. Along the way we spot other boats. Some of the boats have motors, some have oars, and some are barely floating, but they're all loaded with survivors. Rowboats and motorboats and noisy airboats with big props pushing wind, and a flat kind of boat that Mr. Tru calls a "pirogue." "Cajun style," he explains. "Cajuns know the water. So they helpin', too. Is all good."

The boat people wave and we wave back, but Mr. Tru steers away, paddling with a purpose. "Can't play no hero game," he explains warily. "Got all we can do to rescue ourselves."

We glide along, and for a while the only sound we make is the paddle slipping into the water, pulling us forward. The sun burns a hot white hole in the sky. Bandy sits in my lap as if hypnotized, never barking or whining. It's kind of uncomfortable, but I can't push him away, not after what we've been through. I wonder what a dog sees. Does he see a city crushed and ruined, with rows and rows of wooden houses dissolving into the flood, and roofs like sad, broken party hats? Or is it a blur of things he can't quite figure out except for the smell part? A mind-wrinkling stink of rot and mold and garbage and smoke, and something worse, something I'd rather not think about. Maybe Bandy knows, and that's what makes him so quiet.

Far in the distance a siren wails and wails. I've never heard a sound so lonesome.

Malvina says, "Tru? What you say about dry land and a phone? That mean we can call my mom?"

He lifts the paddle out of the water, pausing to consider the question. "We get a message to her, let her know you okay," he decides, finally.

"Promise?"

"Do my best."

Makes me wonder what that means, exactly — get a message to her — but I don't ask. Not my business, that's for sure.

Brightened by the prospect of a phone call to her mom, Malvina keeps up a steady commentary as we glide through the neighborhood. "Oh, I know that house! Old lady, Miss Henderson, she own it till she die, and now it gone to her nieces, with all they kids, and they made it two houses, up and down. And over there, that rusty roof? That a store, they sell food in the back, dirty rice and kettle fry? Real tasty. Owner, he let us buy candy for a penny even though it supposed to be a dime. They got good sno-balls, too."

"Sno-balls," Mr. Tru says. "Oh, yeah, I remember. Cold enough to freeze yo t'roat."

"Uh-huh, it hurt good. And over there, that was Salon Elisha. Lisha, she do my mom's hair. When I was little she had a parrot in a cage that say, 'Who dat?' First time, I thought it was a person in the other room, that's how good that parrot talk. You know Lisha, Tru, she most as light skin as Zane?"

He shakes his head and chuckles. "Boy won't be light skinned for long, with this sun and no hat."

Malvina points. "See over to there? Around the corner from Miss Henderson, you can't see it now 'cause the water too deep, I used to know these twin girls, one year older than me, we sing on this karaoke box they had, with a pink microphone? We pretend like we auditioning for *American Idol*."

Malvina goes on and on, describing everybody that lived in the neighborhood, all the family connections, hardly pausing to take a breath. She talks different from me, like she says "doe" instead of "door," and "stow" instead of "store," and "troot" instead of "truth," but I understand her pretty good. It helps that she talks with her hands, shaping the words, but mostly I get it because she wants me to. My own mom would say she's full of beans, but for all I know that's an insult in New

Orleans. You might better say she's full of sparks. You know how sparklers can burn you sometimes, but you don't mind because the sparks are fun? Like that.

"You like jokes?" she asks, and without waiting for a reply goes, "What kind of dog keep the best time? A watchdog! How you make an egg roll? You push it! Where do bees go to the bathroom? At the BP station!"

The jokes are really dumb, and I've heard most of them before, like in fourth grade, but the way she tells them, so pleased with herself, you can't help but laugh.

The jokes may not be funny, but she is.

"What the judge say when a skunk walk into the court-house? Odor in the court! What you call a pig that does karate? A pork chop!"

"You killin' us, dawlin'," Mr. Tru says, smiling indulgently. "Girl want to be a stand-up comic, but she better not stand up in this canoe!"

"Good one, Tru!" she says. "Next joke, here it come. Which side of the leopard has the most spots? The outside!"

"She on a roll, watch out."

"What do clouds wear under their shorts? Thunderpants!"

"Easy, dawlin', you gone hurt yo'sef like you hurtin' us."

"We gotta laugh, right, Tru?"

"Oh yeah, for sure we do. Go on and drink some water, dawlin'. Bottle there behind you, see it? Zane? You best have one, too."

The mood changes from funny to scary all at once. I'm sipping at the warm plastic bottle, wishing it was cold, when the dirty floodwater ahead of us starts to wrinkle. That's what it looks like at first, like a wrinkle when you shake out a blanket. Like a bunch of wrinkles tangled up together, but moving on their own.

"Keep your hands inside," Mr. Tru says in a warning tone.

The fear hits like something electric, shooting up my spine and into the back of my neck. Lots of people are afraid of certain things. For instance my mom is totally afraid of spiders. Whenever she sees a spider she makes me get it out of the room for her. I don't mind because spiders don't scare me, they're kind of interesting with their webs and all. What does scare me, long as I can remember, is snakes. And there are snakes in the floodwater. Dozens of snakes, uncountable snakes, all writhing together.

Makes me want to scream, but I can't.

"Keep hold a that dog," Mr. Tru says. "We gone sit real still, let 'em pass on by."

Bandy growls deep in his throat but I hold him still as the water around the canoe boils with snakes. Some as thick as my wrist, others as small around as my little finger, but all of them undulating and angry, as if they'd like to bite one another, but they can't tell where one snake ends and the next begins. Heads and tails all knotted up like a slithering mass of oily ropes. Coiling and uncoiling in a frenzy, thumping soft and wet against the sides of the canoe.

I want to close my eyes and wish them away, but I'm too scared not to look. Just when it seems the worst is over a glistening tail slips up over the side and the rest of the snake curls itself out of the water and into the bottom of the canoe, neat as you please.

The snake has a thick, scaly body and shiny black eyes and a white mouth with fangs like white needles. The open mouth is an inch from my bare toes, as if tasting the air, or maybe smelling how afraid I am.

Something touches my shoulder. Mr. Tru with the blade of the paddle, silently urging me to be still. He gives me a tight smile, and then in one deft move he slips the paddle under the snake and flips it high in the air, out of the canoe.

16.

Smoke on the Water

An hour or so later I'm still a little shaky inside, like there's a cold place where a snake has slithered into my brain and won't go away.

"Very unusual," Mr. Tru says about the incident. "Big mess of cottonmouth all up together? Must be the flood drove 'em crazy. Never seen such a thing before, likely won't see it ever again."

He's trying his best to reassure me, saying how rare it is for a snake to come into a boat. But if it can happen once it can happen again, right? And next time he might not be so quick with his paddle. So I keep seeing wrinkles in the water and tensing up. And he keeps on paddling, slow and steady. We pass away from the drowned neighborhood into a wide place with a couple of big, wrecked barges laying half-submerged. The shipping channel, he says. And on the other side of the shipping channel the flood only comes up to the lower windows of the houses instead of the roofs.

Mr. Tru says the water is no more than three or four feet

deep and he could get out and walk the canoe along if he had to, but me and Malvina beg him not to, and that's when I realize that despite all the joking around she's just as scared of snakes as me.

"Stay in the boat, Tru," she pleads. "Stay in the boat!"

He promises he won't get out until the canoe bumps into dry ground. "Come to that it don't have to be zactly dry," he adds, musing. "Soggy will do."

"How long we get there?" Malvina wants to know.

"Long as it takes. But I 'spect before this day end we find us a good place."

Maybe we would have, too, if it wasn't for the smell of a cookout, which comes along about an hour later. Bandy sniffs it first, lifting his head and making hopeful little whines in the back of his throat. Then we all nod pretty much at the same time, and Malvina goes, "Smell that? Somebody grillin'."

"Uh-huh. You can see where they at," Mr. Tru says, pointing with his paddle.

Thin white smoke rises behind a brick school building. The school is on high enough ground so there's only a few inches of water pooled around it. I'm a thousand miles from home, but somehow it seems so familiar that it could be my own school, right down to the old sign posted by the main entrance that says *All Visitors Must Sign In at Main Office.*

Mr. Tru paddles over, nudging the canoe up to the front steps. That's the first time I notice his foot hurts, because as he gets out of the canoe he grabs his leg and grimaces in pain.

"Tru!" Malvina cries.

"Ain't nothing, dawlin'. Sore foot is all. Bumped it a little when the flood came." He takes a deep breath, forces a smile. "You wait here while I check it out."

He limps through the door, into the school.

So we sit there waiting, smelling that hungry smell. Pretty soon my stomach starts growling, and it growls so loud and so long that Bandy perks up his ears, as if he thinks there's another dog somewhere nearby.

Malvina gets to giggling and can't stop. "You real funny, ya know that?" she says. "Sound like you gots the Lion King in yo tummy."

It is pretty funny, if you think about it, how your body makes noises whether you want it to or not — some of them way worse than stomach growls — so I get to laughing, too, and Bandy joins in with a couple of happy yips.

We're still laughing when Mr. Tru limps out of the school.

"You ain't gonna believe this," he says.

Inside, the school smells kind of moldy and damp. But that's only like the bottom layer of all the smells. The top smell, the cooking smell, gets stronger and stronger as we head toward daylight at the end of the dark hallway. The fire doors have been propped open to a paved area behind the school, with an old rusty basketball hoop at one end. On the pavement, lined up like cars revving at a stoplight, are three gas cookout grills with delicious-smelling smoke pouring out from under the covers, and a bunch of folks crowding around with big smiles on their faces.

These are the first happy faces I've seen since before the hurricane, and all those smiles make me want to smile, too. My mom always says a smile is easier to catch than a cold and as usual, she's right.

Mr. Tru takes off his top hat and makes a little bow to the crowd. "Thank you all. Yo hospitality much appreciated."

The people gathered around the grills don't seem the least bit closed off about a few more hungry strangers crashing their cookout. "The more the merrier," they keep saying, handing us plates. What happened is, they've been using a local elementary school as an unofficial shelter. Unofficial because the doors had been locked and they had to break in at the height of the flood, when it was the only dry spot for miles around. With the power out it made sense to empty the cafeteria freezers before the food thawed out and spoiled, so they're grilling up enough chicken wings and fish sticks for the whole neighborhood, or those that stayed behind. Those that couldn't evacuate, or chose not to, and managed to survive the wind and the rain and the rising waters.

Mr. Tru asks if we can make a few calls, but the phones are dead here, too. "Cell towers got blown out like everything else," one of the men explains. "On the radio it said they got some landlines still good in Gretna, and could be some cell reception out to Jefferson, but who knows? Most of the city flooded, that's what they say. Gentilly, Metairie, Treme, Ninth Ward, St. Bernard Parish, all underwater."

Mr. Tru nods to himself, as if this confirms what he suspected. "Levees failed," he says. "Nobody did nothing to fix them old levees. They mostly nothing but dirt and they finally failed."

"Ya bra, they fail. We in the flow now."

"Police?"

"Ain't seen no po-lice. Ain't seen no National Guard. Ain't seen no Red Cross. Nuh-uh. We on our own."

Malvina gets quiet in the company of all these adults, barely parting with her name when asked, and I realize she's pretty shy around strangers. Which is kind of a surprise, considering how talkative she's been with me and Mr. Tru. But even so, she's not so shy that she won't dig into a plate heaped with grilled chicken wings, quietly urging me to do the same. "Better feed that lion, boy," she whispers.

Bandy's having a good time, too. He doesn't stray far from my side, but people keep coming over and feeding him little scraps and saying what a good dog he is, which makes him shiver with pleasure. After a while I kind of get it that talking about my dog is an excuse for people to check me out. Probably wondering what a light-skinned New Hampshire boy is doing in this particular neighborhood, with these particular people, although they're too polite to ask directly. Mr. Tru mentions about my great-grandmother, and how Gerald Dupree was my father, but nobody around here seems to know them, and the local folks sort of pull back, not wanting to push the subject, which is fine with me.

Finally Malvina leans over, speaking low. "Maybe you an alien dude from outer space. Got the ears for it. Like Mr. Spock."

My hands automatically check my ears, which are mostly under my hair, and then I realize she's laughing softly, her sparkling eyes full of mischief.

"Got me," I say, dropping my hands.

"Oh, you easy," she says, giving me a little bump with her skinny shoulders.

Thinking about it later, after all the bad stuff went down — and the good stuff, too — that's the moment when me and Malvina started to be true friends. Sitting there eating our fill and joking around like we'd known each other for years. I even ate some fish sticks, which normally I hate, because she says New Orleans–style fish sticks are really good as long as you got some dipping sauce, and they did, in little plastic packets like from McDonald's only way better.

We eat until we can't swallow another bite and I'm starting to feel pretty good about everything. Like now that it's over all the scary stuff that happened was really just part of an exciting story I can tell my friends, and soon the phones will start working and I'll call my mom and tell her to come get me, and everything will be fine.

That part, the feeling-good part, ends when this fearsome-looking dude with designer shades and thick gold chains slides up to us and goes, "Well now, this a soo-prise. Malvina Rawlins, as I live and breathe. Too bad about yo momma."

Malvina looks at him the way she looked at the snake that slipped into our canoe.

17.

Bad Trouble

This one time I was riding home on my bike and a doe stepped out of the woods and just stood there, motionless. The sun was setting and everything sort of blended together, the woods and the leaves and the little speckled deer and probably me on my bike, too. Maybe that's why the doe didn't bolt back into the woods, because she thought standing completely still would make her invisible. It's like that with Malvina when the fearsome dude mentions her mom. She freezes. No expression on her face, like she's hiding somewhere deep inside herself.

Right away Mr. Tru comes over, a look of concern on his face. "What's going on? You say something 'bout this girl's momma?"

The dude in the cool shades and gold chains, he smiles, showing his strong white teeth. "Look who it is," he says. "True blue Trudell, the trumpety man! You in luck, Tru, that I happen to run into you and the girl."

"You scaring Malvina. That ain't right."

The man moves a little closer. He's not that much taller than Mr. Tru, but he's twice as big around, all edge and muscle. "I ain't scare nobody," he says, very quietly. "All I do, mention how unfortunate it is that her mom can't be here to look out for her. Which is tragic, you know? On account of her situation."

"What you want?" Mr. Tru says, looking worried.

The man picks something from his teeth, flicks it away with his little finger. "You awares who I am, old man?"

"Got an idea."

"Then you already know me and Malvina's mom, we have some interest in common."

"She work for you," Mr. Tru says grudgingly.

"Naw, naw. Nothin' formal. Person do me a favor, I do them a favor, like that. When Malvina's momma went away I wonder where her child might be at, case I could be of use, you know? But it like she disappear. They say you want to find something, stop lookin' and there it be."

So far Malvina hasn't said a word. She stares at the ground, not at the man, not at nobody.

"What you want?" Mr. Tru says again.

"What I want? Ain't about that. It about Dylan Toomey doin' a favor for a friend. You flooded, right? House gone? Nowhere to go? I'm a fix you up. Get you a dry crib, give you food, clothes, TV, anything you need. Let me watch over you and the girl, make sure you all come to no harm."

Mr. Tru starts to say something but thinks better of it. He looks smaller, like the air has gone out of him somehow. After a moment he says, in a real meek voice, "Might be for the best, Mr. Toomey. We, um, we can sure enough use a roof over our heads."

The man in the shades looks satisfied. "Good. We take care of yo situation soon we done here." And then he saunters back to the grill, holding out his plate for another helping. Everybody making room for him, being extra careful not to step on his toes or offend him in any way.

Mr. Tru crouches, smiling around at everybody but talking to us in an urgent whisper. "Malvina? Zane? We in trouble, children, bad trouble, and we got to move quick. Get ready now. You ready? I'm a go make a fuss and when I do, you all run for that canoe, fast you can."

Malvina says, "What about you, Tru?"

"I catch you up. Don't look back, just go!"

He stands, real casual, nodding and smiling like everything is okay. Heading for the grill as if he wants another helping, too, and that's when he seems to trip over his bad foot and sprawls, knocking over one of the grills.

Everybody screams.

Me and Malvina, we're gone before the smoke clears. Heading full speed back into the school, racing through the long, dim hallway and out into the bright sunlight. Me praying that nobody has stole the canoe. And they haven't, because there it is, battered and green and beautiful.

Malvina leaps into the front, with Bandy right behind her. I give the canoe a shove and manage to climb aboard without tipping us over. Then Mr. Tru explodes out of the door, running and limping at the same time as he keeps hold of his battered top hat. Yelling, "Go! Go!" he drags himself into the rear of the canoe.

We're maybe fifty yards clear of the school, paddling hard, when Dylan Toomey saunters out, the sun glinting off his gold chains. Pretending to dip a toe in the water and then recoil, he grins like this is all a big joke, like he can't be bothered to chase us, not if it means getting wet.

Then he gives us a little wave and shouts, "See y'all next time! That a promise!"

18.

Come Hell and High Water

After paddling like mad for a mile or so, Mr. Tru takes a pause, sliding the canoe out of sight between a couple of half-sunk cars and a building that was turned sideways by the flood. Branches reach out of the water from drowned trees, some of them with leaves still green, as if a crazy, junkyard jungle has started to sprout from down below.

We haven't said barely a word, none of us, since we made our getaway, but you can tell Mr. Tru is trying to decide about something. It feels like we're all stuck between one second and the next and can't take a breath until the clock ticks over. Finally he goes, "Dawlin'? Time we told this young man the troot about what he got hissef into."

Malvina avoids looking at me. Instead she fusses over Bandy, scratching his ears. The little dog whines, like he's trying to understand why the humans are acting so stiff and weird, and finally I go, "It's okay. Really, it's none of my business."

"You part of it now, like or not," Mr. Tru insists. "Malvina?"

She folds her skinny arms across her chest. "My mom got arrested and sent to rehab," she announces in a flat voice, staring out at nothing. "She an addict."

"She gone beat it this time," Mr. Tru says softly.

"That what you always say."

"Have faith in your heart, dawlin'. Your momma love you more than anything."

Malvina shrugs, like she's heard this all before and it can't touch her anymore.

"Rehab doin' its work. Your momma getting well. You see."

Malvina only looks away.

"That man back at the school, Dylan Toomey?" Mr. Tru says. "He a local drug boss. Like he say, he done Malvina's momma a few favors, if givin' her drugs is a favor. And when she got arrested in possession, and they send her to rehab instead of jail, might be he's worried she say somethin' to the po-lice about his bidness."

"My momma ain't no snitch!" Malvina says defiantly.

"She do the world a favor, lock up a gangsta like him. And you know that, dawlin'." He glances at me. "So, Zane, you understan' why we leave? Why we had to make our run?"

I shake my head. "Not exactly. I mean, he's a scary-looking dude and all that, but it seemed like he was trying to help us."

Mr. Tru nods. "Oh, I can see how it might appear that way to you. But he intend to help hissef, not us."

"By giving us food and shelter?"

He shakes his head. "Nah, nah. No gift. Man don't give

nothin' away. Always a price. Dylan Toomey, he worried. If Malvina's mom have to choose between going to prison and coming home to her child, she choose her child. She love you, dawlin'."

The heat and stench of the floodwaters makes our eyes sting, so I can't be sure if Malvina is crying or just blinking away the sweat.

Tru sighs and says, "If Toomey get hold of Malvina, and keep her under his evil eye, then her momma don't dare say nothin' to nobody about his criminal ways. See, he own a bunch of fourteen-year-old boys, dealing his dope on the corners. Malvina's momma know the name of every boy. What you think happen to Dylan Toomey when the po-lice hear that? You understan' now?"

"Yeah," I say. And I do, sort of.

"I promised her momma I'd keep her safe, come hell or high water. Ha! High water already come, but I'm tryin' a keep us safe as I can. Malvina?"

No answer. From the set of her mouth it's obvious she's done talking. She sits as still as can be, like a carved mermaid on the bow of a boat. A skinny black mermaid with electric hair, and salty tears dripping from her chin.

Mr. Tru paddles us out into the harsh sunlight of the afternoon, resuming the quest for dry land and a safe place to stay. "Zane Dupree? Guess you figured out by now, you dint get rescued by no Red Cross!"

19.

A Patch of Grass

This one time on my birthday, the year we got Bandit, I'm fooling around with the new puppy and my mom gets this funny look. She goes, "That is so weird. I just heard your dad," and I say something stupid back, like there's no such thing as ghosts, and she goes, "It wasn't a ghost, Zaney, it was the way you laughed."

That's when she told me the story of how she met my father. She was in the Air Force and had to go to this promotion party for someone she barely knew, and she was trying to figure out how to leave without being impolite when she heard this dude laughing in another room. Had no idea who he was, but something about the way he laughed made her want to see what he looked like. So she excused herself and went and saw my dad yucking it up with a couple of his friends. "We looked at each other and we knew, from that very first moment," she said. "The funny thing? Your father was a really serious guy. He didn't laugh all that much, okay? But he did that night."

"And the rest is history," I said, smart-mouthing her.

But she got me back by saying, "You know what? That's something your father would have said."

Which basically left me speechless. I mean, what do you say to that? It's not like I hate my father or anything. You can't hate someone you never knew, even if he did something stupid like get himself run over by some old gumby before you were born. But it's weird knowing part of me comes from a dead man who grew up here in New Orleans. A dead man who was once exactly my age, and who looked at this place through eyes not much different from my own. Except that he wasn't a stranger here. He had family and history in New Orleans, he had a brother that died here. This was his home till he ran away for whatever reason. My father must have known these neighborhoods like I know my neighborhoods back in New Hampshire. He probably rode his bike down this very street, except it wasn't underwater then, and old people hadn't been left behind to drown or die in the awful, stifling heat.

Anyhow, for some reason that's what I'm thinking as we glide along, paddling straight into the hard, sun-blasted shine of dirty water, and the sky smeared with smoke. What would my father make of all this? Would he understand it better than me? Because, to be truthful, I don't really get what happened back at the cookout, or if Dylan Toomey is really as fearsome as he looks, or if we really needed to run away. But I do understand one thing. Something powerful is happening, even if I can't quite see it. Something bigger than the storm, bigger than the ruined city, something awesome and terrible, rising up from destruction.

I've got this awful feeling the bad stuff isn't over.

Along in the late afternoon we come upon a different neighborhood, where the houses are a little bigger and farther apart, and the dirty mark left by the flood never comes much over the front steps. The water isn't but a foot deep, barely enough to float the canoe, and when we start scraping bottom Mr. Tru gets out and tows the canoe up behind some bushes.

Me and Malvina and Bandy scramble out of the canoe, onto the soggy ground.

"Best we stretch our legs," Tru says. "And I bet that dog needs to do his business."

Which he does, with a grateful look.

"Good boy, Bandy."

"Keep hold his collar," Mr. Tru advises. "Don't want him runnin' off wit no pack a wild dogs."

"Bandy'd never do that."

"Call of the wild," he says, cocking an ear. "Hard to resist."

Off in the distance dogs are barking, and they do sound wild and probably vicious. So when Malvina hands me a little coil of yellow rope from the canoe, I tie it to Bandy's collar and wrap the end around my wrist. Better safe than sorry. And it's not like he's never run away.

The patch of grass we're standing on leaks water with every step, like the whole city, even the dry part, has become one big sponge. Heat rises from the damp ground, a heat that steams you to the bone. And to make it even more miserable, swarms of mosquitoes feast on us.

Malvina, swatting at them, goes, "You know why these bugs are like the Red Cross? 'Cause they want us to donate blood," and grins at her own joke.

"Don't tell me about no Red Cross," Mr. Tru responds, frowning. "They gone. Evacuated and left us to our troubles."

He swats at the mosquitoes with his top hat, eyes all squinted up behind his clunky black-framed glasses. We're on dry ground, more or less, like he promised, but he doesn't look all that happy about it. "Got to be careful hereabouts," he says uneasily. "This a place don't take kindly to strangers."

"Looks like everyone got away," I observe, glancing at the boarded-up doors and windows of the big, stately homes.

"Maybe so," Mr. Tru says. "Or maybe they hidin'."

"What we do?" Malvina wants to know.

He shrugs wearily. "Knock on doors and hope for the best," he says.

20.

What Shines in the Fierce Sunlight

We don't actually knock on doors because Mr. Tru is worried about what he calls "possible booby traps." So he calls out to each house from the street, "Anybody home? Can we get some help?!"

It's pretty obvious that Mr. Tru doesn't feel comfortable in this neighborhood, or for that matter begging for help from strangers who won't show their faces. So he stands in the street, a respectful distance from each house, cupping his hands to his mouth and calling out. When no one responds we move on. House after house. Greeted by silence, and sheets of plywood nailed over windows like closed eyelids, blind to everything.

Sometimes we hear motors running from behind the houses. Generators. That means people, right? But none are willing to show themselves, not to us. It's a lonely feeling, thinking that some of the owners might be in there, hiding behind the plywood. Not that we know for sure, although Bandy barks at certain houses, as if he can sense life within. More than once I see something flit in the shadows behind the shutters, as if a person moved out of the light, away from our sight.

"Folks scared," Mr. Tru mutters under his breath, like he's trying to convince himself. "Why else they ignore us? A man and two child, presenting no threat to none of them?"

Some places, if you ignore the torn-up shrubbery scattered around like dirty confetti, and a few trees leaning over to touch the soggy ground, you wouldn't know there'd been a hurricane or a flood. The houses in this part of the city are mostly untouched. Big sturdy homes built on higher ground, with maybe some leaves clotted into the intricate trim of front porches, like spinach stuck in their front teeth.

We're most of the way down the block, and the houses keep getting bigger and grander and more closed up, some with steel hurricane shutters pulled down like shades, when Bandy stops in his tracks and starts growling deep in his throat.

"What he sense?" Mr. Tru wants to know.

A moment later we humans hear it, too. The low thrum of an approaching helicopter. I expect to see a flash of orange and white from the Coast Guard, but that's not what passes overhead, blasting hot wind from above. This helicopter is smaller, darker, unmarked. After it slips over the horizon we hear the engines throttle down, the whine of the blades quickly subsiding.

I don't know much about helicopters, but it sure sounds like it landed somewhere in the neighborhood.

"Might be they come to save us!" Malvina suggests.

"Might be," says Mr. Tru doubtfully.

Malvina starts to run off in the direction of the helicopter and Mr. Tru hollers at her to hold up. She turns back, looking hurt at the sound of his raised voice.

"Mercy, child," he says, much softer. "Can't keep up wit you runnin' like that."

He's been limping pretty bad since we got out of the canoe, wincing with every step. Whatever he did to his ankle or foot, it appears to be getting worse. Not that he'll talk about it, except to say it ain't nothing to worry about.

Malvina takes his hand, and for a moment she looks younger than she is. "I gone stay close by you," she promises.

He takes a deep breath. "We check on this, if nothin' come of it we get back to the canoe, find us a safe place to shelter, dry or not. That the plan."

"That a good plan, Tru."

He grins and shakes his head. "You got me all confused, dawlin', being so agreeable." He turns to me. "Zane Dupree, you keep hold of that dog. Some folks round here will shoot a stray dog, they see it off the leash."

"Yes, sir."

So we keep together. Mr. Tru limping and not wanting any help, not even a shoulder to lean on. The girl with the wild hair holding his hand, and me with my dog on a leash of borrowed rope. All of us simmering in the unbearable heat, tormented by endless mosquitoes, and desperate for a helping hand.

Doesn't make sense that no one is willing to help us. Folks were helping survivors get out of Grammy's drowned neighborhood, like me and Bandy got rescued from the attic, okay? Why not here, where the storm barely did any damage? Is there something about big houses with fancy trim that makes people hide from those in need?

In the distance we hear sharp, echoing bangs that could be gunshots. Malvina shrinks against Mr. Tru, and he groans as the weight comes down on his foot. "Pay no heed," he says, as more shots go off like muffled firecrackers. "Long ways gone. None to do wit us."

We trudge along, Bandy tugging eagerly and me holding him back. Fearful of those gunshots, if they are gunshots. But what else makes that noise? So what are they shooting, out there in broad daylight? Maybe firing to signal they need help?

"Best not to dwell on," Mr. Tru says.

Maybe Malvina has it right, maybe the helicopter has come to rescue us. It's not like we need so much. Shelter from the sun, water to drink, and a phone to call my mother. Oh, and a doctor to fix Mr. Tru's foot.

Truth is, right now I'll settle for the phone. This may sound kind of weak, but I miss my mom something awful.

"We gone far enough," he says, heaving a sigh. "Time to turn back."

Malvina drops his hand and skitters ahead, trying to see around a pile of thick-leaved branches that have been piled in the middle of the street like a green barricade. "There it is!" she exclaims. "Come on, Tru, lean on me, we almost there!"

I pull down a branch and take a look. At first I'm not really sure what I'm seeing. Because the way the helicopter shines in the fierce sunlight, it might be a giant insect. A glittering dragonfly perched in the garden next to a white, three-story house. A house so big it has tall columns holding up the roof. A mansion, like you see on TV. On one side of the mansion are enormous, moss-covered trees, untouched by the storm, and on the other a wide lush garden that has been flattened either by Katrina or the downdraft from the helicopter itself.

The blades of the helicopter are still turning and the elegant machine whines like a dog begging to be let off its leash. Me and Malvina want to run into the garden, see if they have room on the helicopter, but Mr. Tru holds us back. And a good thing, too, because a moment later men swarm from the house. Men in matching green polo shirts and baggy camo pants. Men wearing mirrored sunglasses and carrying shotguns.

The guns swing in our direction, until all you can see is the black holes at the end of the long barrels.

"Hands up! Down on your knees! Now!"

Have you ever tried raising your hands and dropping to your knees at the same time? Not the easiest thing to do in the world, and Mr. Tru has the most trouble getting down. He's trying to lower himself without hurting his foot when one of the shotgun men plants a shiny black combat boot on his chest and shoves him to the ground.

"You leave him alone!" screams Malvina, launching herself at the man with the boots.

He peels her off the way you'd flick at a bothersome bug, and hands her to me. I can feel her heart slamming in her chest, and the tightness of her anger.

"Keep hold of this little hellion," he commands. "As a legally contracted security force we have the right to defend this property from the predations of looters, using whatever force deemed necessary. Meaning we can shoot you dead. And that's exactly what's going to happen unless you answer my questions. You, the light-skinned boy! Look me in the eyes, son. No hemming and hawing, no lies, are we clear? You lie and I'll know. This is my lie detector, right here."

He smiles an evil kind of smile, touches the end of the shotgun barrel to my chin, and says, very softly, "Bang. You lied."

21.

Like an Animal Crawling Away

It's not like I've never seen a shotgun before. In New Hampshire lots of kids have deer rifles and shotguns, and they go hunting with their fathers and uncles. Shooting deer and ducks and like that. But I never had a shotgun aimed at me. Certainly not by a man who sounds like he's looking for an excuse to pull the trigger. I should be deathly afraid — and part of me is — but mostly it doesn't seem quite real. Like I'm in my own personal movie, playing the victim, and any minute the director is going to yell, "Cut!"

Bandy believes it, though. He's flat on his belly, whimpering. To be truthful, I'm more afraid they'll shoot my dog than me. Grown men don't shoot unarmed boys, right?

Right?

"Who else is with you?" the man demands, prodding me with the shotgun. "Simple question, boy. You scoutin' for your 'posse' or your 'crew' or whatever you people call 'em?"

The question doesn't make any sense. All I can do is shake

my head in confusion. From the ground Mr. Tru says, "Just us, suh! We 'lone."

"I'm talkin' to the boy."

But Mr. Tru insists on speaking, despite the shotgun aimed at his head. "We found him in a attic, him and that little dog. Boy from up north, he don't know nothin' about nobody in New Awlins. No gang, no posse, no crew, nuttin' like dat."

"Is that a fact."

The man looks down the long gun into my eyes, his forefinger caressing the trigger guard.

"Boss," another man says. "He's only a boy."

"Boy can murder and steal just like a man."

"They're unarmed."

"Uh-huh. Maybe they hid their weapons in the bushes."

"We checked, boss. Nothing."

Boss Man lowers the shotgun. With a smirk on his face he turns to Mr. Tru. "So you just a sad old man with two orphan chillun, is that your story?"

The way he says "chillun," he's obviously making fun of Mr. Tru, who shakes his head and looks away.

Malvina pipes up, defiant. "Hey mister, why you so mean?" she asks. "Must be something wrong in your brain, to make you so mean."

Boss Man ignores her. "Here's the question," he says, concentrating on me and the old man. "The moment of truth. Are you all as ignorant as you look? You expect me to believe you don't know what's going on out there?"

On his knees, Mr. Tru says, "We know what the flood done. That's what we tryin' to 'scape from."

"Uh-huh. And you just so happen to ''scape' into a wealthy parish. Rich homes for thugs to rob and steal."

Mr. Tru shakes his head. "Ain't no thug! Ain't no thief!"

"People on the rampage, looting whatever they can carry. Stealing from honest folk, you don't know anything about that?"

"No, suh."

"We ain't steal from nobody!" Malvina says hotly.

"Malvina, you hush now," the old man says, looking at the guns. "This on me."

"People resentful of what others might have. So they rise up when the opportunity presents itself. In this case a flood."

Mr. Tru lifts his chin. "We're not looters," he says. "We lookin' for help is all."

"Everybody know Tru!" Malvina says, protesting. "Trudell Manning ain't no thief, he a famous music man!"

Boss Man rolls his eyes. "A musician. God help us. I suppose that explains the hat."

Another man approaches. "Boss? We about done here? Pilot doesn't want to stay any longer if he can help it."

"Cargo loaded?"

"One more rug," the man says. "But it might put us over the weight limit."

Mr. Tru hears this and says, in disbelief, "Rugs? That what this all about, rescuin' some kinda *rugs*?"

Boss Man says, "For your information the owner has a very valuable collection of Oriental carpets. Hired our service to protect them from the likes of you."

Behind him, the men in green polo shirts drag a rolled-up carpet from the big house and carry it out to the waiting helicopter.

"Leave the rug and take these children," Mr. Tru suggests.

"So they can sabotage the helicopter, is that your plan?"

"No ways! I'm asking you, suh, to do the right thing. Never mind me, long's you do right by these children."

Boss Man says, "Our mission is to secure the premises and remove the inventoried carpets. Mission accomplished. Contract fulfilled. We will not be deterred from our purpose. Your kind want a free ride in a shiny helicopter, apply elsewhere."

The old man sighs and shakes his head in disgust.

Boss Man doesn't like his attitude. He uses the end of his shotgun to push the hat from Mr. Tru's head. Then he steps on it, crunching the hat under his boot heel.

Mr. Tru freezes, not reacting, except to warn us with his eyes. *Don't do nothing, keep you still.*

We all of us, including Bandy, keep still.

Grinning at our fear, Boss Man says, "A squad will remain on the premises, fully armed and ready to respond with deadly force. Is that understood?"

We nod silently. He turns and marches to the waiting helicopter.

As the big machine takes off, the downdraft from the screaming blades blows Mr. Tru's straw top hat over the flattened grass, like an animal crawling away with a broken spine.

22.

Leave a Message, Please

So that was when I started to really get it, how one bad thing can lead to another. The first bad thing might be, say, a hurricane, and it crashes into the world and starts other bad things happening, like the power going out, and trees crushing houses, and then the levees fail and the water rises and suddenly a million other things are going bad all at once, and some people are suffering, and some are dying, and some are helping, and others are acting wicked superior and pleased with themselves, like Boss Man with his shotgun, trying to make us feel small and stupid.

I figured they were all like that, the team of private security guards in matching green polo shirts and camo pants and shiny black combat boots, but as usual I'm wrong. Because we're a couple of blocks away, moving slow to keep pace with Mr. Tru, when one of them hurries to catch up with us.

"Hey, wait! I got something for you all." He holds out a bulky gym bag. "Isn't much but what I could grab. Water, some canned goods, like that."

Malvina's face is as tight as a clenched fist. "Oh yeah," she says with a sniff. "*Now* you tryin' to help. Probably some kinda joke, makin' fun of us. A bag of rocks or somethin'."

The man unzips the gym bag, revealing bottled water and tins of tuna and canned goods. "The boss, he can be a real jerk, okay? Obviously you're not criminal types, but he can't see it."

"He sees we po' and black," Mr. Tru says.

The nice dude nods in agreement. "Oh yeah he does. But the boss, he's right about one thing. This area is no place for strangers. We're not the only security team on the ground in this parish. There are others, less disciplined. Trigger happy, you might say. Plus some owners have holed up, armed to the teeth and intent on defending their property. Trust me, everybody is stressed. You don't have to be a looter to get shot on sight. Any stranger will do."

Malvina goes, "Why you work for a man like that, if you ain't mean like him?"

The nice dude shrugs. "It's a job. All I'm sayin', keep moving." He turns to leave.

"Hey, wait up," Mr. Tru says, as if he just remembered something important. "Got you a cell phone?"

And that's how I finally get to call my mom. The nice dude keeps looking behind him, worried about Boss Man, but he allows me to use his cell. The connection is full of static and it never rings, exactly, but suddenly my mother's voice is going, "*Zaney, if that's you, leave a message, honey, please?*"

Then a beep sending me to voice mail.

I turn away to hide my tears. Thinking, *Zane Dupree, you total moron, you've been wanting to call home for two of the longest days that ever there were, and when you finally get the chance you can hardly keep from bawling like a baby. Totally demented!* But somehow I calm down enough to leave a message on Mom's voice mail, which is that me and Bandy are okay and this nice old guy, Mr. Trudell Manning, is helping us, me and this girl, Malvina, and we got a canoe, and I'll call again as soon as we're someplace safe, and not to worry, and how sorry I am for being so dumb about everything. And then I can't talk anymore and Mr. Tru gently takes the phone and hands it back to the nice dude, who marches away without a backward glance.

Bandy, catching on to my mood, pushes his nose against my leg, wanting to be petted, and that helps some. Also Malvina starts cracking these lame jokes to make me laugh, and that makes it even better.

Stupid stuff like, "Why the teacher cross her eyes? She couldn't control her pupils! What you call a train loaded with gum? A chew-chew train! Why do dogs run in circles? 'Cause it hard to run in squares! Why the turkey cross the street? 'Cause he wasn't chicken!"

Bandy gets pretty excited, hearing us laugh, and somehow I let go of the rope around his collar. He's off like a shot, legs a blur as he races back to the big house, like he can't wait to return to the scene of the crime. Barking like a maniac, as if to let them know he's coming.

I try to make a grab for that skinny yellow rope, but Mr. Tru grips me by the arm, hard enough to hurt.

"No," he says, very firm. "Keep by me."

"They'll shoot Bandy!"

"Might shoot you," he says. And then adds, gently, "Dog will come back on his own. See if he don't."

Bandy streaks on like a ground-hugging missile, the rope flapping from his collar. He skids past whatever he's headed for, kicking up clods of grass and dirt. Then he picks something up in his grinning mouth and races back and drops it at Mr. Tru's feet.

"Pretty good dog," he admits, picking up his battered top hat.

I wrap Bandy's rope around my wrist, and vow never to drop it again, hat or no hat.

By now Mr. Tru is limping so bad he's got no choice but to rely on me and Malvina for balance. She's dragging the gym bag of goodies, I've got the dog, and Mr. Tru is leaning on our shoulders. We're keeping to the middle of the street so nobody can accuse us of trespassing.

He advises us not to look at the boarded-up houses we pass along the way.

"You see a crazy man in the street, you don't meet his eye, lest he throw his fear on you," Mr. Tru explains. "Same thing applies in this case, 'cept the crazy men are hiding inside their own homes, intending to shoot anyone comes too close, or looks too interested. We get back to the canoe, we gone stick by the flooded area from now on."

"Uh-huh," Malvina says. "Gone find you a foot doctor, too."

He doesn't respond to the suggestion, exactly, but he doesn't fight it, either. "I'm tending to the notion of Algiers," he says, changing the subject. "We'd have to cross the river, with the dangerous currents and all, but I got this cousin in Algiers, Belinda? Her place might be dry. It higher where she at, I know that much. Ain't seen her in some time, we both busy and all, but we on good terms."

"Whatever you say, Tru, that's what we gonna do."

Takes a while, but we make it back to where the houses aren't quite so big and the ground leaks water at every step, and crazy-sounding dogs are still howling off in the distance. Back to where we pulled the canoe out of the water. We can see the skid mark it made in the soggy grass as we came ashore.

What we can't see is the canoe, because it's gone.

All the Way Dark

Glaring at the boarded-up houses, Mr. Tru says, "One of them stay-behinds musta took it." He cups his hands to his mouth and shouts: "That my canoe you stole! My own canoe, bought and paid for!"

His powerful voice echoes through the neighborhood. In the distance the crazy-sounding dogs bark a little higher, but from the boarded-up houses, nothing but the steady hum of generators.

Malvina collapses on the gym bag, skinny arms resting on her knobby knees. "Ain't fair," she says, so furious her eyes are practically glowing.

Meanwhile Bandy plops his head on my feet with a heavy sigh. Like if we want him to move from this spot he'll have to be carried. Which is not going to happen. "I think we should get out of here," I say, my own anger rising. And fear, too. Fear of what might happen if we stay.

The old man gives me a thoughtful look and nods in

agreement. "I expect you right. Folks'd steal a canoe from the likes of us, who know what they do once the sun go down?"

"Ain't fair!" Malvina repeats.

"Get you up, dawlin'," he says, voice going soft. "Fair don't figure. What's done is done."

She takes his hand. "Where we go now, Tru?"

"Where I been tryin' to avoid. The Superdome. The mayor, he say don't even think about going to the dome lest you got nowhere else. 'Shelter of last resort' he call it. Ha! 'Last resort' mean they got no food, no water, no beds, no nothin'. Last time, Hurricane Georges, I think it was, the dome got tore up and trashed real bad. But since we been deprived of our transportation, we got no choice: we got to stop there for a night. Be okay. Somebody at the dome bound to help this boy find his family. We rest up to get our strength, then you and me, dawlin', we cross the river and go on to Algiers, visit with my cousin. Belinda's a real nice woman, she run an animal shelter, there by her house. I expect she'll give us shelter, too, till we get on our feet. So, you with me on my plan?"

"I'm with you, Tru."

"Thank you, dawlin'."

He takes a deep breath and we set off, away from the big white houses and the shotguns and the stealers of battered old canoes.

"Easy now, one step at a time," he says. "Got us a good plan, we gone be okay."

No choice but to keep moving, slow as that might be with an old man limping, and two kids trying to hold him up, and a little dog that doesn't understand why the humans are so unhappy. Our eyes stinging with the stench of filthy flood-water, bugs eating us alive in the fearsome heat.

The true fact is, I never felt so miserable or hopeless. But Mr. Tru says if we get to the Superdome there might be help.

Might be.

We keep to the soggy edge of the floodwaters, winding through blocks of small, drowned houses. Some crushed to soggy splinters, some tipped from their cinder-block founda-tions, as if the muddy ground wants to swallow them up but can't quite choke them down.

The stink is so awful it hurts, and Mr. Tru says there must be dead bodies trapped inside some of the houses, but there's nothing we can do about it. "Their troubles over," he says softly. "They in heaven now."

"Heaven smell like that? Eww!"

"Show some respect, child."

"Why nobody come to get 'em?"

"I don't know, dawlin'. World gone crazy I guess. 'Nother block we have a little rest, okay?"

On the next block the stench isn't quite so bad. Just regular garbage smells. The sky is dirty, too, with plumes of ugly smoke, and everywhere you look there is wreckage from the flood, like some monster barfed up all the garbage in the world and coated it with mud and slime.

Progress is slow. Partly because the flood doesn't leave us a straight path, and partly because Mr. Tru can't hardly walk. His ankle is swollen up to about twice normal size. Every step makes him groan in pain, although he tries to hide it.

"Pay no heed," he says, wincing. "Ain't as bad as it looks."

Oh, but it is. Probably much worse, according to the worried eyes behind his clunky, black-framed glasses.

"Maybe we could get some ice," I suggest. "My mom sprained her ankle once, and ice cubes made the swelling go down."

He chuckles. "Good idea, but ice cubes be rare as icebergs in New Awlins in this heat, with the power out."

"They had some ice in the coolers back at the school!" Malvina says excitedly. "We could get some of that."

"Uh-huh. We a long way from that school. And a long way from Dylan Toomey. Least I hope we is."

"I could sneak in," she offers. "They never see me."

"Sure you could. And you an angel to offer. But we closer to the dome. Maybe they got ice at the dome. Or least-ways a doctor fix me up. Now, you children stop worryin', hear me? Old Tru been through worse and he get through this, too."

We keep going, but real slow, and not just because Mr. Tru is limping so bad. The ruined streets, all the junk and damage, make the going difficult, and we're still finding our way through the wreckage as the sky starts to dim.

Night is coming, and fast.

Malvina says, "Where that dome? How far we go, Tru? It gone be all the way dark soon. And no streetlights."

"You right, dawlin'. Takin' longer than I expect. Guess we best find a place to rest our bones."

"I'm afraid of them houses, Tru," says Malvina, her voice hushed.

What she really means is she's afraid of the dead bodies that might be inside.

Me, too.

We start looking for shelter, keeping away from the scary houses.

"See over that way?" Mr. Tru says. "Maybe try that."

He indicates a small garden shed that's washed up on the shore of the floodwaters. Tilted a bit, but more or less intact. An old thing with plywood sides and a battered metal roof. Big enough to hold, at most, a lawn mower or two. And that's exactly what's inside, an old push mower and a bunch of rakes and shovels and just plain junk.

"Ain't exactly home sweet home," he says.

"We fix it up, good as new," Malvina says, sounding determined.

Mr. Tru keeps hold of Bandy's leash while I drag the mower and rakes and stuff out of the shed. Malvina gets busy with a shovel, clearing out the stinky mud. She's moving so fast I can't hardly keep up with her, and by the time the last of the daylight fades from the sky we're jammed inside that little shed. Three people and a dog, and glad to be there. Glad to be anywhere other than out in the black darkness of the drowned city.

Huddled inside the shed we can't see one another's faces, but that doesn't matter. The shed is good. There are less bugs than outside and it feels safer to be hidden away for the night. To tell you the truth, Malvina isn't the only one scared of the dark. The dark wouldn't be scary at home, in my own room, but in the heat of a drowned city the darkness is like something alive, rubbing up against you. Or worse, something dead.

Stupid thoughts! *Get real, you moron. The real stuff is bad enough without being spooked by stupid scenes you remember from stupid horror movies. The only thing coming to get you tonight is hungry mosquitoes. Keep that in mind. And be glad you're not alone.*

"We good?" says Mr. Tru.

"I'm fine," I say. "You?"

"It's all good. Tomorrow gone be better. Has to be."

Malvina hums a tune as she roots around inside the gym bag, cans clinking.

"Suppertime," she announces, pressing a plastic bottle and a tin can into my hands. The bottle is easy — water — but I don't know what to do with the can. It doesn't have a pop-top lid, so how am I going to open it without a can opener?

Mr. Trudell Manning to the rescue. "Patience," he says. "I got my little knife, if I can reach into my pocket."

In the dark we pass him our cans. He has to feel along the edge, find what he calls the "sweet spot" for the blade on his jackknife. Didn't know I could be so hungry, after all the grilled food I stuffed down at the school, but that was hours and hours ago — seems like days, really — and my stomach is making a fuss by the time Mr. Tru finds my hands and carefully places the opened can in my clutching fingers.

I dip in and find not the vegetables I've been expecting — anything edible would have been okay, no problem there — but the slippery deliciousness of cold raviolis. Okay, not cold exactly, more like air temperature, which is practically hot, but it doesn't matter, because these are the most delicious raviolis ever, in the history of the planet. So good and satisfying that it pains me, physically pains me, to save a few for Bandy, huddled in my lap and waiting patiently for whatever I'm willing to spare.

He nibbles at the raviolis delicately, licking my fingers as he licks the sauce from my hand and makes a contented noise.

"Good dog, Bandy."

But I'm thinking, *Zane Dupree, what a rotten crud you are, not wanting to share with your own dog.*

After we finish eating we're sitting in the steamy dark, kind of quiet for a while. Can't help it, I'm expecting something bad to happen because bad things keep happening to us, and there's no way to know what it will be, the next bad thing, because that's the way it works, I can see that now. That's part of what makes it bad, that you don't know what it will be or when it will happen.

Mr. Tru must have picked up on my dark mood. "I expect you children worried. Troot, I'm worried, too. But no matter what, we stick to the plan. Sun come up, get you to the dome, find a phone that works. People there to help you, bound to be. Zane get with his family, Malvina let her momma know she okay."

"What about you, Tru?" Malvina says.

"I be fine."

"Get you to the dome, they fix you up, right?"

"Uh-huh. And in case I forget, dawlin', after you call yo momma, I want you to call my cousin Belinda Manning in Algiers. Her number listed in the book. Last Chance Animal Shelter, can you remember that?"

"I remember," Malvina says in a very small voice.

"Say it for me, dawlin'."

"Last Chance Animal Shelter."

"And Zane, while I'm thinkin', Belinda knew your daddy, Gerald Dupree, and his brother, James Dupree. At the time we all live in the same neighborhood as Miss Trissy and her boys, and Belinda she just about their age. I'm older, see, so I wasn't payin' much attention to them boys, but Belinda, she knew 'em."

"She knows what happened, how James got killed and why my father ran away?"

"I expect she does. No doubt Miss Trissy tell you the story in her own good time, but in case she don't and you want to know, call Belinda Manning at the Last Chance Animal Shelter and tell her you a friend of mine. Son should know about his daddy, even if he gone. 'Specially if he gone. Maybe you think it don't matter, but it do."

"Okay," I say.

Late in the night I wake up to the sound of a running motor and for a moment I think there's a big car outside. My mom, come to find me. But it's not a motor, it's the old man snoring loud enough to shake the walls of the garden shed. Snoring and moaning a little, between the snores.

"You awake?" Malvina whispers urgently.

"Yeah."

"I been thinking."

"Uh-oh," I say.

"Oh, you funny. Serious, though. You and me, we got to make a promise. Whatever happen, we take care of Tru like he take care of us. Because if his foot bad in the morning, he gone tell us to go on ahead, not to worry none about him, that he be okay. Which he won't. So, you promise?"

"Sure."

"You mean it? Whatever happen, whatever he say, we don't

leave Tru behind. You down with that, New Hampshire boy? You promise on your heart?"

"I promise on my heart."

Her hand finds my hand.

"You my brother," she whispers. "We blood."

24.

Top of the Ten

Next morning, just like she figured, Mr. Tru says the plan has changed and we're to go on ahead without him.

"Get you to the dome, you can tell 'em where I'm at," he says. "They send an ambulance."

Malvina rolls her eyes. "You seen an ambulance? Ain't no ambulance. Forget it, Tru, you comin' with us. Me and Zane, we carry you."

"Naw, naw. That ain't gonna work. Too far. I'm a draw you a map."

They go back and forth like that for a while, one getting more stubborn than the other. Him not giving up on the idea that we should go on without him, and Malvina shaking her head and saying nuh-uh, no way, forget about it.

All the time I'm looking at the girl and thinking, *How did she know?* Then I remember how sometimes I know exactly what my mom is going to say or do, so maybe it isn't so strange that Malvina would guess what the old man was thinking, since she's known him all of her life.

"Dawlin', I promised your momma I take care of you, and that's what I'm 'tempting to do."

"Don't mention my momma! This ain't about my momma! This about me knowing what I ain't gonna do, and that's leave you behind."

He appeals to me, suggesting I should talk sense to her. When I look away and start muttering excuses he goes, "What, oh no, you in this together? You part of this willfulness, boy? No respect for your elder?"

"Sorry, sir."

"Don't fight it, Tru," Malvina says. "We made up our mind."

She gets on one side and I get on the other and together we raise the old man up. He keeps muttering about disobedient children but doesn't fight us too much and we manage to get him clear of the garden shed. Progress is slow, one shuffling step at a time, and Malvina keeps trying to distract us with her dumb jokes.

"Why the tomato turn red? It saw the salad dressing! What did the ocean say to the ship? Nothing, it just waved! Why do elephants never forget? Because nobody ever tell them anything!"

After an hour or so — and it seems like a million years — the old man asks can we stop and rest. As we help him sit down on the curb he almost faints from the pain.

Malvina, hands on her hips, says, "Man needs a wheelchair."

I want to say, *duh, no kidding*, but the fiery look in her eyes keeps my big mouth shut. Then her expression brightens and she makes another stupid joke. "What's a wheelchair? A chair with wheels!"

"Not funny," I say, feeling grumpy and discouraged.

"Not funny," she agrees. "But it might work. Zane, you stay by Tru."

And then she takes off, scampering back in the direction we came from, and soon she's out of sight.

I don't know what to think, except she's gone crazy.

Mr. Tru shouts after her to no avail and then turns to me. "Go with that girl. Make sure she okay."

"She told me to stay."

He snorts. "What are you, a dog? Somebody say 'stay' and you stay?"

"I can't leave you alone. I promised."

"I won't be alone," he says. "That little dog will keep me company."

I hand him the leash.

How do you find your way in a wrecked city when you didn't know the place before it was turned upside down by a flood? Last time I was on my own, before the storm hit, I was following Bandy and he knew where he was going even if I didn't. But on my own, within about five minutes I'm lost. Some things look familiar — we passed that little house with the missing roof, right? Other things I don't recognize, like a bicycle hanging from a spike on a telephone pole. But then I was probably looking at the ground, helping the old man find his way, or anyhow not paying close attention to where we were going.

I'm starting to feel more than a little panicked when I hear Malvina yelling, not far away.

"Come on out of there! Let go! Don't you fight me, don't you dare!"

Her agitated voice is coming from a storefront building. Most of the aluminum siding has been ripped off and the windows smashed, but the sign over the broken door still says *Crescent City Insurance, Home & Vehicle.*

Before running into the building I grab a hunk of wood from the street, fearful that she's fighting with somebody, right? But when I step into the storefront, waving a length of two-by-four, I feel like a complete idiot. Because Malvina is all alone inside, yelling at a tangled pile of furniture that has washed up into a muddy corner.

She's yelling at a chair, actually. An office chair. A skinny girl with arms about as big around as toothpicks, she's struggling to get the chair free from the pile like her life depended on it.

And then I get it, the answer to "What's a wheelchair?" Because this is a chair with wheels, the kind you can scoot and spin around in, like I used to do with my mom's chair at her desk.

I drop the hunk of wood and give her a hand.

"You're really smart, you know that?" I say, tugging at the chair.

The grin lights up her whole face.

*   *   *

The streets aren't exactly smooth, so the ride for Mr. Tru is pretty bumpy, but he's able to keep his bad foot off the ground, and that's the only thing that matters. It's just a dumb old office chair, a cheap one with five plastic wheels, but it makes all the difference in the world. We probably look stupid weaving our way through the streets, a boy pushing an old man in a battered top hat, and a girl dragging a bulky gym bag, and a little dog trotting along behind us, but we don't care. It's like the chair gives us hope that things will get better, if we give them a chance.

The sun is bright, the sky is blue, and Malvina Rawlins is full of beans.

"What you get when you cross a rooster and a duck? A bird that gets up at the quack of dawn! Why are musicians so cool? Because they have so many fans! How you make an egg laugh? Tell it a yolk!"

"How many jokes do you know?" I ask her.

"Too many!" Mr. Tru answers in her place, and we all laugh so hard we have to stop and get our breath back.

We sit there for a while, me and Malvina on the curb and the old man in his chair, looking at us and shaking his head, like he can't believe what he's seeing. "Tall and mostly white," he says. "Short and mostly black. Couldn't be more different 'cept you both got the same grin. Now why is that?"

"'Cause my jokes are infectious!"

That gets us laughing again. When we finally do start moving, Mr. Tru waits until we make it to the end of the block — the buildings aren't quite so wrecked here — and then he raises his arm and points.

"There it is," he says. "Peekin' over the top of the Ten."

By "Ten" he means the elevated highway that cuts through the city. And there, floating like a giant flying saucer in the ripples of heat rising from the interstate, is the roof of the Superdome.

25.

Broken People

Before my trip to Smellyville the most people I'd ever been around was probably the day before Christmas at the Mall of New Hampshire. Mom is really into it and always makes me go. Okay, that's not quite true, because I like it, too, all the sparkly decorations and the fake presents piled high in the store windows, and the trees decorated with blinking lights, and phony Santas with their fake beards and padding, and so-called normal people wearing elf hats and ringing bells, and even the goofy songs they play over and over again in the back ground. But after an hour or two, waiting in lines and stuff, the crowd starts to bother me. Mom says it's about my personal boundaries, but does anyone really enjoy being shoved up against strangers, knowing what they had for lunch because you can smell the salami or whatever on their breath? Eww, right?

Okay, maybe that's stupid, because what's going on at the Superdome is so far from Christmas in New Hampshire that it might as well be on another planet. The closer we get, the more people are wandering around, looking like zombies on a long walk to nowhere. Some are trudging through nearby streets still covered by a foot of water. Some are huddled wherever they can find shade, fanning themselves with pieces of paper or cardboard, their eyes kind of stunned or empty. Some are pushing shopping carts full of stuff they saved from their houses, photo albums and suitcases and clothing and like that. This one guy in a torn T-shirt and pajama bottoms is shaking his fist at the sky and shouting out a tumble of words that don't make any sense, and Mr. Tru suggests we cross to the other side of the street. "Ignore the poor man," he says. "He broken."

There are lots and lots of broken people. Old people, young people, kids, babies. Mostly black folks, but some white people, too, and a few in between who probably look a lot like me. Not that I'd want to check myself in a mirror, not after days without a shower, and wearing clothes that are baked in sweat and soaked in floodwater and crusted with dirt from spending the night in a garden shed.

Come to think of it, me and Malvina and Mr. Tru, we probably look like zombies, too.

The closer we get to the dome, the worse the smell.

Okay, this is really gross, but the whole Superdome reeks of pee and poop. And if the outside is this bad, Mr. Tru says, the inside must be worse.

"All them folks crammed together in this heat? I dunno, dawlin', maybe this dome plan a mistake."

"But they got doctors, right?" Malvina says. "Must be doctors and medicine inside. Somebody fix your foot. Bound to."

"I hope so," says Mr. Tru, but he doesn't sound like he believes it.

When we get around to the main entrance, there are even more people. Hundreds or maybe thousands — too many to count. Some gathered in family clumps and some on their own. Some in wheelchairs or sitting on plastic milk crates. Some are crying and wailing and begging for help and some are drenched in silence. Many are standing in a long, long line that snakes partway around the building and doesn't seem to move.

Men in uniform guard the entrance. City police, some of them, but mostly army-looking dudes with helmets and combat rifles, looking like they'd rather be anywhere but here.

"National Guard," Mr. Tru says. "They in charge."

Looking around at the crazy scene, Malvina says, "Ain't nobody in charge."

She turns to this older woman propped up in a lawn chair, holding a rain umbrella over her head, attempting to shade herself from the sun. All alone with her belongings in a grocery bag at her feet.

"Scuse me, ma'am," Malvina says. "You know if they got doctors inside?"

The woman shrugs. "If they do I didn't see none. Old folks dyin' in there from the terrible heat and no medicine, that's why I come back out to the street. They tryin' to do right, those that can, but there's too many people and not enough National Guard. Some of the young mens getting violent, making threats and smashing up the soda machines and stealing what they can. Got so bad the Guard don't want nobody more inside."

"They closed the dome?"

"Seem like it. Might change their mind, they been doin' that, too."

"Is that why all these people are in line?"

The woman points with her umbrella. "That the line for buses. They keep saying wait for the buses. Buses supposed to take us away, make us someone else's problem. Houston, they say, or Atlanta — anywhere but New Orleans. We been waitin' and waitin', but they ain't no buses."

Hearing the old lady describe the situation, Mr. Tru gets so discouraged he seems to shrink in his chair. He starts apologizing about how he's messing us up, but Malvina cuts him off. "You sayin' this your fault?" she says. "Did you make the hurricane? Huh? Did you make the levee fail? Did you make the flood? This ain't on you, Tru."

"Yeah, it is," he insists. "I should have got you out of New Awlins like they told us to."

Folding her skinny arms in defiance, Malvina goes, "Was that old car of yours broke? Yes, it was. Broke and wouldn't run. Did we have money to get us to Baton Rouge, or rent a motel somewheres? No, we didn't, 'cause you give all yo money to help my momma. Did you save me from the rising water? Yes, you did. So do me a big fat favor and stop sayin' it your fault. *It ain't your fault!*"

She shouts the last part at the top of her lungs. So clear and strong that for a moment everybody in the crowd outside the dome stares at this skinny girl with the wild hair and the big voice. Not the least embarrassed, she looks right back at them and grins. "True dat!" she says, raising her fist, and her words seem to echo through the crowd, repeated from one to the next.

"True dat," they all agree.

Normally it's kind of embarrassing when somebody makes a big fuss in public, but not this time. It's really cool hearing all those strangers agree with Malvina, even though a lot of them probably don't know what she's talking about, exactly.

The crowd doesn't pay attention for long, though. Because a big, booming noise comes rolling down the street. A shiny black Cadillac Escalade cruising along with wicked rims and a sound system that makes the ground shake under our feet. So loud you can feel it in your chest, rattling your rib cage.

I recognize the song because it's been playing everywhere all summer: "Lose Control" by Missy Elliott.

Boom, boom. Boom, boom.

Chrome pipes, outta sight. And sure enough, the Escalade has chrome pipes and blue lights and mirrored windows tinted the deepest shade of dark.

Boom, boom, shaking the air, shaking the earth.

The Escalade stops beside us. A rear door opens, and out of the cool leather interior slips a scary-looking dude in designer shades and gold chains.

Dylan Toomey, big as life.

26.

A Big Pile of Stink

Okay, I'll admit to being scared stiff. Like my feet are glued to the hot pavement even though I want to run away. When something bad comes your way, something you can't fight, that's what you're supposed to do, right? Run for your life? And Dylan Toomey is something bad. First time, back there at the cookout, I wasn't sure — he made it sound so tempting, a nice dry place to stay, and TV and games and stuff — but this time there's no doubt. I get this awful cold feeling in my guts at the idea of him taking charge of Malvina. And that's clearly what he intends to do. Standing cool on the street, like the heat doesn't exist, at least not for him, and ever so casually stroking a thumb along his gold chains, his cool shades reflecting the Superdome.

He makes a sign with his left hand and the music stops, although the Escalade stays running. Waiting.

"Malvina!" he says with a big smile. "Honey, we been lookin' all over. Your momma worried sick about you."

Malvina says, "How you know that?"

"Just talked to her," he says, displaying a cell phone. "Had us a long conversation."

"You did not!"

Sensing trouble, people in the crowd start shuffling off or backing up, wanting nothing to do with the gold-draped dude with the cool-rim SUV.

Something is about to go down and everybody knows it.

Toomey grins and saunters closer. For him all the thousands of survivors in the vicinity of the Superdome might as well not exist. Even me and Mr. Tru don't exist for him. He's entirely focused on Malvina, the way a cat focuses on a chipmunk that chatters back.

"Don't you dare!" Malvina says, raising her voice. "I ain't go with you!"

Dylan Toomey keeps on coming, taking his time.

That's when I notice we've attracted the attention of the National Guard. They react reluctantly, but one of them says something into his walkie-talkie, and then another one nods. The pair of them warily take up new positions, holding rifles at the ready. Not interfering yet, but keeping an eye on the situation.

Mr. Tru says, under his breath, "Time you both get runnin'."

He's gripping the arms of his chair, ready to launch himself at the man in the gold chains.

Malvina, seeing what's about to happen, steps away from the chair and raises her arms, as if to distract attention from the old man. "Somebody help us!" she screams. Not like she's afraid, more like she's angry. "This man ain't no family to me. He a gangsta! He a thug!"

Toomey reacts with a smirk, confident that no one will risk interfering. Smiling this fake smile, he reaches out as if he wants to take hold of Malvina and lead her to the safety of his shiny SUV.

She ducks under his outstretched hand and screams, "He got a gun! He got a gun!"

Everything happens all at once, and it seems like in slow motion even though it's not. The National Guard dudes react by taking aim and shouting, "Drop it! Drop it!" and "Show us your hands!" and "Get on the ground!" pretty much all at the same time.

Toomey kind of freezes in place, although he's still smiling. I can see, even if the Guards can't, that his hands are empty.

While all this is going on — my heart doesn't have time for more than one beat, that's how fast everything is happening — Malvina grabs my arm and somehow I know what she wants me to do even though she doesn't say anything. Mind melding, my mom calls it.

Whatever it is, I know.

I put Bandit in Mr. Tru's lap and without saying a word we take hold of the old man's chair and run it along the street, fast as we can, never looking back. Just flying. Mr. Tru holds on for dear life, bouncing around as the little plastic wheels blast over the pavement. Bandy hunkers down, his ears flat. Behind us the National Guard dudes are freaking out and screaming at Toomey not to move or they'll shoot. We're running as fast as we can and I expect to hear gunshots but they don't shoot and nobody tries to stop us getting away, either. In fact people are making room, opening up places for us to run and then closing behind us, either on purpose or by accident, it doesn't matter so long as we can keep running, shoving that chair over the rough pavement.

We're making a pretty good getaway, all things considered, but there's no way we can outrun that Escalade if it wants to catch us. Malvina must be thinking the same thing, because after we go a few blocks, out of sight from whatever we left behind, she comes to a stop and goes, "We need a place to hide!"

A place to hide. Oh yes. That's my urge, too. If I could lift up an edge of the sidewalk and burrow into the earth, I would. But there's no place to go, no place to hide. All around us are boarded-up office buildings and a few vacant lots that are blown so bare there's not even a tree to hide behind.

"Maybe they'll arrest him," I say. "Maybe we're safe."

I don't believe it and neither do they. Mr. Tru goes, "That man slippery as a snake. Even if they put cuffs on him, he'll send somebody after us."

"Zane? Can you take that plywood off the windows?"

I make a quick inspection. "No way. Even with a screwdriver it'd take forever."

"Okay," she says, taking a deep breath. "We keep runnin'."

That's when I notice this huge Dumpster alongside one of the office buildings. A nasty green thing overflowing with piles of garbage and trash, spilling out into the street and leaking in all directions.

"You serious?" she asks, her nose wrinkling.

"It can't smell worse than the Superdome."

Oh, but it does. Imagine a thousand backed-up toilets, and ten tons of fresh steaming dog doo, and a hundred dead cats, and all the dirty cat boxes for all the dead cats, and every spoiled rotten thing from every nasty garbage pail in the world.

The Dumpster stinks worse than that.

Way, way worse.

And it's not like we climb into the Dumpster or anything. There's no room inside because it's overflowing, okay? We're only hiding behind it, behind the piles of rotting garbage. Gagging on the smell, eyes watering from the overwhelming stench. Even Bandy keeps shaking his head and snorting through his nose, like he can't believe a smell this strong.

It seems like forever, but really it's only a few minutes later that we hear the *boom, boom* of the SUV rolling down the street with the sound system blasting. The deafening bass rattling off the buildings and making it twice as loud.

Boom, boom. Boom, boom.

"Lose Control" by Missy Elliott.

Man, I'm starting to hate that song.

I peek around the corner of the Dumpster. There it is, the gleaming black Escalade with the wicked cool rims and chrome pipes. The Escalade looks like it has muscles of steel and throbbing light.

This time Dylan Toomey doesn't even bother to get out of the car. A back window rolls down. His face hangs in the interior dimness like a shadow of a moon.

He smiles, flashing gold.

The music stops.

"Malvina Rawlins!" he bellows. "Aw right! You a smart girl, juss like yo momma! I like that! Sic the Guard on me and run off, that was smart. And now you hiding behind that pile of stink, assuming I don't want to get my new Jordans all dirty. And you right! Got better things to do on this fine morning. Got me a business to run, folks to take care of!" Something about what he says strikes him funny, because he chuckles and shakes his head in amusement. Then he tips up his shades so we can see his clear, cold eyes staring at us like brown laser beams. "I be watching you, little girl. Wherever you at, wherever you go, I be there. We gone get together soon, you and me. We gone be friends, you see."

The window slides up, like a cloud sliding over the moon, and a moment later he's gone, riding *boomba-rattle-boom* out into the ruined city.

27.

Stupid Water

Algiers, Algiers," Mr. Tru keeps mumbling. "Get you over to Algiers, Belinda help us."

If you didn't know better you might think the old man had been drinking, because of the way he slurs his words, but the scary fact is, he's not drunk, he's sick. Bad sick. Sick with fever from his foot and ankle, which have turned all purple and swollen up to about twice normal size. We're pushing his chair down the middle of the street, what Malvina calls the "neutral ground," with the sun blazing and the heat rising from the pavement and yet poor Mr. Tru is shivering.

"Little Belinda," he mutters to himself. "She a good one. Oh yeah, mighty good."

"We find her, Tru. Don't you worry. Everything gone be okay," Malvina tells him. But the tears streaming down her face tell a different story.

Can a person die of a bad foot? I don't know. Maybe, if there's no one to take X-rays, or give medicine, or the normal stuff they do. Or maybe it's that he got infected from the bad water, or a snake bit him and we didn't know it.

I never felt so stupid or helpless, wandering down that street, not knowing where to go or what to do. It gets so bad I almost wish Dylan Toomey would find us, so I wouldn't have to think about anything, or make decisions.

Malvina says, "You take the chair, I'm a go ask where we go."

She stops people in the street, asking where to find a hospital or emergency room. This one skinny dude says, "Hospitals, they all backed up or flooded out," but when Malvina insists, he points us in a certain direction. "Maybe you find what you need," he says, doubtfully, and then he's gone.

We follow his directions for a few blocks, and come to the edge of the floodwater. From the nasty look of things it has gone down a little, but the water is still way too deep to push Mr. Tru along in his wobbly chair.

If we had a boat or a canoe, maybe. But we don't.

Bandy barks at the stinky water.

"Come on, boy. Leave it alone."

He looks up at me and I swear he shakes his head in disgust. That's how bad it is, when a dog who slurps from toilets turns up his nose.

Back to the big wide street where dazed survivors huddle in the shade, looking stunned. Back to inquire again where we might take a sick old man. Most people just shake their heads, or mention someplace north of the city, too far away to make sense. Others say the Superdome, where we've already been, and know how bad it is, with too many sick and not enough medical help. Someone else tells us the local hospitals have all been flooded, and have their hands full trying to evacuate patients by helicopter.

"They been forced up on the roofs, you know? First floor underwater, so they lost power. No electricity, no machines to keep folks alive. Somebody tell me the Red Cross comin', with clinics and nurses and all, but I ain't seen 'em yet."

Malvina finally finds a policeman, a black man in a blue uniform sitting in a broke-down patrol car that won't start. The cop looks about ready to cry, turning the key and nothing happening. He tells her pretty much what the other dude said about the hospitals being flooded and overwhelmed, and that maybe we should take our chances at the Superdome.

Same old story.

After a few more futile attempts the cop gives up, leaving the patrol car with the windows down and the door unlocked. He walks away from the car and from us. Malvina calls to him but he doesn't look back.

After the cop scurries out of sight this one guy comes over and hands us a bottle of water. "Plenty of fluids," he suggests. Then, taking a closer look at Tru, he adds, "Might better pray."

Which makes Malvina mad, the suggestion that the old man is so far gone. "Never mind what he say — you tough, Tru. You gone make it! Go on, drink!"

The bottle drops from his trembling hands and Malvina kicks it. "Stupid water!" she shouts, and people shy away from us, sensing trouble.

"Hey," I say.

She jumps on the bottle with both feet, crushing it. "Stupid! Stupid! Stupid!"

After she settles down I go, "So what do you want to do?"

She wipes her eyes. "Only thing left," she says. "Go to Algiers like he want."

"How do we get there?" I ask.

"I don't know," she says. "But I'm pretty sure we have to cross the river."

When we ask which way to the river, everybody points in the same direction.

28.

Wonder Dog

We're not the only ones who want to cross the river out of New Orleans. There are lots of other survivors heading in the same direction, staggering out of the city across that bridge. A few in slow-moving vehicles, but most on foot. Most of us filthy and exhausted and desperate. My first thought, as we push Mr. Tru up the long sloping incline, is that it's like some scene from a movie about the end of the world. Like we're all fleeing an alien invasion, except instead of invading Martians we had invading water.

Give me a Martian any day.

Whatever, it sure feels good to be leaving Smellyville. The darkness seems like it has lifted and Malvina is back to her old joking self.

"Why the one-handed man cross the street? He want to go to a secondhand store! Why wouldn't the cannibal eat the clown? Because it taste funny! What kind of ship never sinks? A friendship!"

Mr. Tru perks up. "That last one a good one," he says.

"Soon's we cross over we find somebody fix your foot."

"I believe you will, dawlin'. You can do anything you put yo mind to."

"Soon as you fixed you be marchin' in the band, blowin' yo brass."

"Oh yeah? And where you be?"

"Dancin' in the second line!"

It does my heart good to hear the two of them bantering again. Maybe Mr. Tru is getting better on his own, although you can't tell it from his foot and ankle, which are still swollen bad. At least he's not shivering in this heat and it has to be a good sign that he's looking around and paying attention, right?

He points and says, "Zane, young man, do you see how the river curves? That why they call us 'The Crescent City,' 'cause the Mississippi River makes a bend in the shape of a crescent, and inside that crescent, that New Awlins. River curve along like you see, then head north for a little ways, then turn all the way south. That direction over there? That where we came from, and you can see the whole neighborhood still underwater. See them roofs poking up like the fins of a fish? One of 'em might be my house."

It's true. Being up on the bridge gives us a perspective on the size of the disaster. The flatness of the floodwater shines like a dull mirror all the way out to the edge of the horizon. The city, miles of it, is mostly underwater, with some bits poking up here and there. But the flood won, that's for sure. Below us the river is swollen and clotted with wreckage. Pieces of broken houses, every kind of garbage and junk swirls slowly along as if the whole thing is a giant, backed-up bathtub trying to empty through a blocked drain.

I don't want to look too hard at all the stuff in the river. You never know what you might see.

"We all whistling past the graveyard," Mr. Tru says, tapping the brim of his beat-up top hat.

I've heard my mom say the same thing and never really knew what it meant. Now I do. Except instead of whistling, Malvina is telling a steady stream of stupid jokes, and the old man chuckles at all of them, no matter how dumb.

"What has four legs and a arm? A happy pit bull!"

"Oh, you a terrible child."

"You think that bad? Try this. Why do elephants have trunks? Because they look silly with glove compartments!"

"You right. That silly."

"Yeah, but you laughin'. How you make a hot dog stand? Take away its chair! Why do birds fly south? Because it too far to walk!"

"We walkin' south, dawlin', mo' or less."

"You ain't walkin'," she points out. "You ridin' in style."

Some of the folks trudging over the bridge know Trudell Manning from his music, and say how good it is to see he survived, and how they expect to hear him play again when he's ready.

"My brass all gone," he says with a shrug. "House, too."

Not complaining, just stating a fact.

And it hits me. When this is finally over I'll be able to go home to New Hampshire, to the house I grew up in, but all of these people, thousands and thousands of them, have lost everything. The flood has taken it all.

After we get across the river the ramp gradually curves down, heading for ground level. The closer we get to the end of the ramp the more we're squeezed over to the side by the cars going by, jammed full of passengers and belongings. Which I guess is why no one offers us a ride, because they're already full.

At least that's what I tell myself.

Finally we get to a place where the road widens out for a row of tollbooths, and that's where our progress slows to a halt. There are a lot of folks in the way, and cars weaving around them, and at first I can't make out what is going on, or why we've stopped.

"Road is closed," I hear someone say, but that doesn't make sense because there are dry streets below us, a whole neighborhood that appears to have escaped flooding.

Why would the road be closed?

Malvina is not in a mood to be slowed down. "Comin' through," she says, pushing on Mr. Tru's chair. "Make room. Scuse me, but we comin' on through."

Me and Bandit follow along behind her. The dog is in my arms so the yellow rope doesn't get tangled in the chair or under my feet. Actually he's the one who lets me know something is wrong, because suddenly his little body tenses and his ears lay back. "What's wrong, boy?" But by then the crowd opens and I can see for myself.

A bunch of cop cars are blocking the tollbooth area, lights blinking. And standing behind the cop cars, a bunch of cops with shotguns. This one cop with a megaphone bellows, "TURN BACK, BY ORDER OF THE SHERIFF'S DEPARTMENT. THIS EXIT IS CLOSED TO PEDESTRIANS. YOU WILL NOT BE ALLOWED TO ENTER THIS PARISH. TURN BACK NOW."

At first I'm shocked, but then it kind of makes sense because everywhere we go there seem to be men with guns, wanting to keep us out, at least those of us on foot. As vehicles approach the blockade the cops talk to the drivers and let most of them drive on through, but they won't let any of us walk past the tollbooths. Like we're being punished for not having cars, for looking ragged and desperate and poor.

"THIS EXIT IS CLOSED TO NONRESIDENTS. TURN BACK NOW."

Malvina goes, "No way."

Mr. Tru seems sort of confused, like he isn't sure where he is. "There must be a parade," he says. "Is there a parade?"

Malvina re-grips the back of his chair. This skinny girl with arms like toothpicks. "We the parade, Tru. We goin' through them tollbooth."

"I dunno, dawlin', it don't look right."

"It ain't right," she says, and pushes him through the crowd, into the open. Heading for the blockade of cop cars, and all the men with shotguns crouched behind, looking nervous.

*   *   *

Thinking about it later, maybe I should have stayed back, me and Bandy. Maybe they'd have let her through if it was just her and a sick old man in an office chair, one of the wheels spinning around like it's on a crazy shopping cart. Maybe me and the dog looked threatening and that's what set them off. Or maybe it didn't matter one way or another and they were trying to make an example of us, demonstrating they were in charge.

But what happened, happened. I can't get away from that.

"HALT. TURN BACK. THIS EXIT IS CLOSED."

Malvina keeps pushing. Moving so determined, so ferocious, that I have to hurry to catch up even though my legs are way longer than hers.

"STOP. THIS IS YOUR ONLY WARNING. TURN BACK OR WE WILL FIRE."

She keeps going.

I get close enough to hear Mr. Tru say, "This ain't no parade, dawlin'. Might be we should go home."

"We goin' home, Tru," she says defiantly.

Malvina keeps going, that crazy wheel spinning. Me with the dog following close behind. The hair rising on Bandy's neck, and mine, too. Both of us wound so tight it feels like we're going to explode.

And then cops in armored vests swarm from behind one of the cop cars, taking aim.

"STOP. THIS IS AN ORDER."

Malvina shoves the chair forward, as if she's trying to ram through the barricade, as if she and Mr. Tru are going to get past the tollbooths or die trying.

The men lift their shotguns, tracking us.

Taking aim.

That's when Bandy explodes from my arms. Baring his teeth and growling like he intends to tear the ankles off anyone who threatens our new friends. He leaps at the men with guns as if he's a big bad wolf instead of a twenty-pound mutt.

A shotgun explodes. I can feel the punch of air and the bright heat of the flash. And then Bandy is slammed to the pavement like he's been hit by a shovel and he isn't moving.

Because they shot him, there on the bridge, the men with fear in their eyes. They shot Bandy the Wonder Dog, the best and bravest dog that ever lived.

29.

If a Good Dog Dies

Next thing I'm on my knees cradling him and there's blood all over. His eyes are open but he's not barking or whining or anything, which seems like a very bad sign.

I start screaming at the cops, and at the whole rotten world. Bandy's teeth are bared and his eyes are unfocused and distant. His face is a grimace of pain. His right paw looks like raspberry jam. He's dying. There's nothing I can do to stop it.

"It was an accident," someone says.

One of the cops, I don't know which one.

In the background Malvina is shouting, "You shot my friend! You shot my friend!"

I notice she says "friend," not "dog." Which I'll never ever forget.

I'm watching the light dim in Bandy's eyes when a stranger pushes her way through the ring of cops, telling them to get back, she's a doctor. One of the cops makes the mistake of saying, "It's only a dog, lady." And this woman glares at him like she's the sun and he's an ice cube about to melt. She's a short, round, black lady with chocolate skin and close-cropped frizzy hair and round glasses that make her eyes look as big as brown eggs.

"This is my family," she announces firmly. "You will step back and give me room to treat my family."

And they do, they step back, all these cops with their shotguns and shiny black boots and bulletproof vests. Nobody says a word. Even Malvina keeps quiet while the woman places her hand on Bandy's neck and nods to herself, as if she knows exactly what must be done and how to do it.

"Keep pressure on the wounds," she instructs me. "We have to move fast."

She asks the cops to help her make room in this rusty old van she has. It's loaded up with empty dog kennels and cat carriers. After setting some of the cages on the curb, the cops help Mr. Tru into the front passenger seat and me and Malvina get in the back with Bandy.

A moment later the cops wave us through the tollbooth.

"Belinda," the old man says, "I didn't know you was a doctor."

She snorts. "I'm not. But you *are* my family. That part was true."

You probably figured it out right away. The round woman with the air of authority is Mr. Tru's cousin Belinda. Turns out she had evacuated the animals in her animal shelter to this place outside of Baton Rouge and was on her way back to check on her house in Algiers, which as it turns out is one of the few areas that didn't flood when the levees failed. She's waiting on the traffic to get through the tollbooths when she sees what she describes as "this big fuss on the bridge."

"Didn't know who it was until I recognized that crazy hat of yours," she says.

"This my lucky hat," he says, holding it up by the battered brim.

"Lucky? Are you serious?"

"I'm still here, ain't I? And it brought you to us, didn't it? But it won't really be a lucky hat 'less you save that little dog."

"I'll do my best," she says.

She reaches over the seat and hands me an elastic band. "Put that around his leg, just below the joint. Then wrap him in that insulated blanket, the one by your feet."

All I can do is nod and obey.

Seems like forever, but probably within a few minutes we're in the driveway of this gray cinder-block building with frosted-glass windows and a neon sign that says Last Chance Animal Shelter. Next thing we're in the building and Belinda drops her keys on the counter.

"Follow me," she says.

Bandy's wrapped in the insulated blanket, but he's shivering as I gently place him on the metal examination table. The light is dim — the electricity is out — and Malvina holds a flashlight as Belinda bustles around, chatting as she goes.

"Okay, okay. Here we are. Here we be. The dog is Bandit, correct, and you're Zane Dupree from New Hampshire? I got that much. Trudell says Trissy Jackson is your great-grandmother, correct? Small world, I knew your father, Gerald. Okay, now to business, here we go. First, lift up the edge of that blanket, I want to check Bandit's heartbeat."

She places a stethoscope on his chest and listens, eyes squinting slightly. "Not bad, considering. He's going into shock. Can't stop that, but we can keep him warm and make sure he doesn't dehydrate while we deal with his wounds. You are this dog's guardian, is that correct? Fine. Excellent. In the interest of full disclosure, I am not a veterinarian. The vet who volunteers at this shelter is presently in Nashville, visiting her family. But I am an RVT, a Registered Veterinary Technician, licensed in the state of Louisiana, and I've learned a thing or two over the years. Now — and this is important — do I have your permission to treat Bandy to the best of my abilities?"

I nod permission.

"We'll take it one step at a time," she says with a reassuring nod. "Step one, start an IV. Step two, administer sedation. Step three, clean and treat Bandit's wounds, which are multiple and serious. Young lady, Malvina, is that correct? Yes? Can you continue to hold that flashlight? Excellent. Zane, would you please go back to the reception area and make sure Trudell is okay? Give him water, make him comfortable. Malvina and I will take care of Bandit, and then we'll see if there's anything we can do for Trudell's foot. Lots of footwork today, but that's okay, we can handle it. And Zane? Don't forget to breathe."

I never knew waiting could be so hard.

In the waiting area Mr. Tru has propped himself in a chair. He tries his best to distract me with stories about his little cousin Belinda that lived next door, in the other half of what he calls a "camelback house" on Charbonnet Street, not far from my great-grandmother's house, and how little Belinda started rescuing animals when she was a small child and then made it her life's work. Some of his stories are funny, especially one about a kitten and a parakeet, but all I can think about is *Bandy, Bandy, Bandy.* How much I had always wanted a dog and how long it took me to persuade my mother to let me have one. I kept asking and Mom kept saying no way, I wasn't old enough to take care of an animal and she was too busy because she works full-time, and like that.

No dog, no way, so quit asking.

But I didn't quit asking. I made it my mission in life to get a dog. I took out books from the library about dog training and dog grooming. Mom kept shaking her head and saying books are great but she wasn't about to change her mind. If I couldn't clean up my own room how was I going to clean up after a dog?

So I cleaned my room. I mean really cleaned it, okay? Not just picked up all my stuff but vacuumed everything and even washed the windows.

That really shocked Mom, that I'd wash the windows, but

she wouldn't change her mind. So then I went online and found the results of a medical study proving that owning a dog improved your health. Mom rolled her eyes. "I wish you'd put all that energy and brainpower into your schoolwork," she said, "instead of wasting it on something that's never going to happen."

So I did, and I got A's that semester, and a note from my teacher saying I was much improved. Mom was so totally amazed that for once she didn't know what to say, and that's when I got down on my knees and raised up my hands like they were paws and barked, "*Arf! Arf!* I'm a dog and you'll love me, promise promise. *Arf! Arf!*"

That was it, she caved. Although I didn't know it for sure until the next week, my birthday, when she woke me up early and said, "Rise and shine, young man, we don't have all day," and we drove to the SPCA and there he was, this eager little ball of black-and-white puppy fur that crawled up into my arms and licked my face.

Bandy, short for Bandit. He knew his name right away. Every time I said "Bandy" he'd bark and wag his straight-up tail, like *Yes! That's me!* Mom said I could have called him "Dirt Bag" and had the same result, but right away she loved him, too, because you can't not love a puppy. And when she saw him following me around, not letting me out of his sight, she said, "He's your dog, that's for sure. Bandy belongs to you and you belong to him, and don't you forget it, young man!"

Not that I ever could.

So I'm waiting and waiting, my brain full of *Bandy, Bandy, Bandy* and after about a million years Belinda finally comes out of the examination room with a smile. "There's an old saying, 'when a good dog dies the angels cry,'" she says. "I'm happy to report there will be no crying today."

Takes me a while to speak, but finally I swallow hard and go, "So he'll be okay?"

"Affirmative," she says. "He had several shotgun pellets embedded in his chest and he lost part of one paw, but a dog can get along on three legs almost as good as four. Especially a dog as low to the ground as Bandit."

Mr. Tru puts on his battered old top hat, tugs it firmly into place, and gives me a big grin.

"Told y'all this was my lucky hat," he says.

30.

About My Father

We carry Bandy into Belinda's house, next door to the Last Chance Animal Shelter, and keep him wrapped in the special blanket. He's really groggy from the anesthesia, and I'm worried he won't wake up, but he does with a little whimper of recognition. I tell him what a brave dog he is, and that he probably saved my life by getting in the way of the shotgun, but he doesn't seem to care about that, he's just happy to see me.

People will say you can't know what a dog is thinking, but that's pure baloney.

Belinda's house is small and tidy, sort of like Grammy's house but modern. She says it would be more comfortable if the power was on, so the ceiling fans could move the air, but I don't care about the heat and the humidity. Compared to what we've been through, this is heaven. For the first time since the hurricane we all feel safe.

Malvina helps Mr. Tru onto a couch so he can rest while Belinda fusses over him and makes him take a dose of antibiotics. The medicine is for large dogs but she says it will work just as well on humans. She tells us he has sepsis, which is blood poisoning, and we'll have to watch his temperature but he's a tough old bird.

"First I'm a dog and then I'm a bird," he says. "Make up your mind."

That inspires Malvina to crack some jokes about dogs and birds. "What happens when it rain cats and dogs? You might step in a poodle! Why do hummingbirds hum? Because they don't know the words!"

She goes on, but the jokes are so bad they hurt. Me and Mr. Tru are used to it by now, but Belinda laughs so hard she has to take off her glasses and dry them on her sleeve. "I do love a sense of humor," she says, catching her breath. "I can't tell a joke to save my life. But tell me, young lady, what were you thinking, taking on the entire sheriff's department?"

Malvina shrugs. "I was fed up, I guess."

Belinda shakes her head in wonder. "Girl, you're an itsy-bitsy thing, but you have the heart of a lioness."

As if on cue, Mr. Tru starts snoring. A moment later Bandy is snoring, too, and me and Malvina get into a fit of giggles because it's so perfect, them snoring away like a pair of chainsaws.

While the two of them sleep, Belinda heats up some water on her outdoor grill and makes yellow rice and beans and the most amazing corn bread in a big iron frying pan. The three of us eat our fill by candlelight. It feels like a dream, a really nice dream where we're not running or hiding or being threatened, and then it gets even better because after the meal Belinda goes out to her van and comes back with a cell phone that was charging on the van battery — this was a surprise, I had no idea — and I punch in Mom's number and this time she answers.

The connection is really bad — the cell only has like one bar — and I don't have time to tell her much, not even what happened to Bandy, but this much is clear. Mom wants me to stay where I am. She's already on the way, she'll come to me.

That's fine. I'm not going anywhere.

I'm feeling really good about how everything is working out until I catch a glance of Malvina in the candlelight. She tries to hide it but her eyes are wet and it hits me what a selfish goon I am, only thinking about *my* dog, *my* mom, *my*self. Me, me, me. So I tell her how sorry I am, that the first call should have been to check on her mother, not mine, and she says, naw, naw, that's not it you stupid boy, she's not crying for her mother, she doesn't care about her mother, her mother can rot in jail for all she cares, she's crying because she's happy for me, that my mother is coming to get me, and because it means I'll be leaving soon and that makes her sad. And if I wasn't a stupid boy from New Hampshire I'd know that a person can be glad and sad and mad all at the same time.

Now I really feel crummy, because I don't know what to say to make her feel better.

Belinda says, gently, "The boy has family here. He'll be back."

Malvina folds her skinny arms tight across her chest and says, defiantly, "How he find me when I don't know where I'll be?"

"Because you'll be here with me," Belinda says. "You and Trudell. This is your home now. I said you were family, and one thing you will learn about me, I always say what I mean and mean what I say."

Belinda puts Malvina to bed, in what she promises will be her room, to fix up any way she likes, and I bring a battery lantern into the living room and lay out some sofa cushions on the floor next to Bandy, who is still sleeping fitfully. Sometimes his legs move like he's running. I hope he's dreaming of squirrels, which he loves to chase, not that he's ever caught one.

Mr. Tru remains fast asleep, too. A healing sleep, Belinda says, covering him with a light blanket and adjusting a pillow under his head, tenderly.

"Trudell was like a big brother to me," she says, her voice a husky whisper. "At times my childhood was very difficult, you understand, but he was always there, a calming presence. I feel bad we lost touch these last few years. My fault, not his. It's a blessing that I'll have the chance to make up for that now."

"He's a cool dude."

"He's a kind and lovely man, is what he is. But you're right, he also happens to be a cool dude. Always was."

There's something about Belinda that makes it easy to ask stuff, because the question pops out of my mouth before I have a chance to think about it.

"You said something about knowing my father?"

She shrugs and says, "I knew him slightly. We lived in the same neighborhood and went to the same schools, but Gerald was a year older than me. The Dupree in my class was the young man who would have been your uncle James, had he lived. That was a terrible tragedy, what happened."

For my whole life I've been telling myself it doesn't matter who my father was, or why he did the things he did, because he was gone before I was born. But it does matter, and I guess I always knew that, way down deep.

"What happened?" I ask.

She looks surprised. "You don't know?"

"My dad never told my mother. She thought he was from Biloxi. And Grammy was going to tell me but didn't have the chance."

Belinda thinks about it. "Maybe we should wait on Miss Trissy. Gerald was her grandson, raised like her own son."

"He was my father."

"Good point," she says. "Everybody in the neighborhood knows the story. Why should you be the only one who doesn't? It's not right to keep you in the dark, after what you've been through. Trudell told me as much. So. Are you ready? Here are the facts as I know them."

Belinda explains that it was an accident. An awful accident. My uncle James found a paper bag on the playground and inside the paper bag was a gun. Stashed there by a drug dealer, that's what everybody assumed. Belinda doesn't know all the details, but James and Gerald shared everything, and James showed off the gun to his big brother, fooling around.

Gerald tried to take it away and the gun went off.

"Those two loved each other," she says, "so everybody understood it was an accident, a terrible accident. There was never any question of Gerald being guilty of a crime."

"If it was an accident why did my father run away?"

Belinda sighs. "I don't know exactly, but it had to do with Miss Trissy. She was broke up bad, you understand, having worked so hard to raise those boys, and I expect Gerald thought she blamed him for what happened. For sure he blamed himself. Must be he felt he had to go somewhere and start over. Which apparently he did, because here you are, with the same eyes and the same smile, and tall for your age like he was."

"So my father accidently killed his brother and then an accident killed him? That stinks."

She nods. "Yes it does. But tragic accidents do happen in this world, all the time. We prefer to think they happen to someone else, but sometimes they happen to us, or to someone we love."

"I hate accidents."

"Understood. You have reason to, more than most. I'm only speculating about your father's motivations, but I do know one thing. You, young man, are no accident. You're exactly who he would have wanted you to be. Now get some sleep. Tomorrow is a brand new day."

There's no way I can sleep, not with so much to think about, but I must have passed out from sheer exhaustion, or maybe relief, because the next thing I know Bandy the Wonder Dog is licking me awake and my mother is coming through the door with a cry of joy. She's driven night and day all the way from New Hampshire to find her foolish son that lost himself in a hurricane, and take him home.

One Year Later

When I look back on it, the only thing I'd change about what happened is this: I wouldn't call the place Smellyville. That was childish, and insulting to all the people who live in New Orleans. Or used to live in New Orleans. So much was washed away in the flood, so many homes and lives, that a hundred thousand people haven't been able to return. One of them is my great-grandmother, Beatrice Jackson, Miss Trissy. She lives with us now, up here in New Hampshire, and has joined a church and sings in the choir. They wrote about her in the paper, about her amazing voice, and the amazing story of her life and like that. There aren't many black people living in this area but Grammy seems to have found them all, and me and Mom are getting to know them, too, which is really great.

As for Malvina, she came to visit this past summer, and that was cool once she got used to it. I talk to her almost every day on the phone and she's doing pretty good, all things considered, and still cracking jokes. The jokes are getting better, too. She lives with Belinda, who has been appointed her legal guardian because her mother came out of rehab and then had to go back, which is sad. Malvina says she doesn't hate her mom, just the opposite, she feels sorry for her and hopes she'll someday get free of the drugs. There's always hope, and in the meantime Malvina is really serious about wanting to have a career in comedy. You wouldn't think that tragedy can be turned into comedy but it can. That's the whole point. Like Malvina says, she has a lot of material. Dead father, druggy mother, what a hoot.

A lot of people wouldn't get it, but I do.

Mr. Tru has been staying with Belinda, too, until his new place is built, in a block of new homes reserved for local musicians, but a lot of the time he's on the road with one band or another, some of them famous like Kermit Ruffins and Harry Connick, Jr., and like that. His friends sponsored this fundraiser in the French Quarter to help him get some new brass and so much got donated that he gave away instruments to all kinds of other musicians, which was a beautiful thing. He and Malvina are still tight. I'm sure they always will be, because he saved her life by risking his, and she saved his by risking hers.

You can't get tighter than that.

In case you're wondering, Bandit made a full recovery. We got him this prosthetic paw that slips over his wounded leg and he can run full blast on all four legs and do everything he could do from before, like chase squirrels. Not that he's ever caught one. Mom says if he ever does he'll make friends with it, and that's probably true.

Oh yeah. Dylan Toomey. This is sad, I guess, but about a month after the storm he was killed by one of the underage kids who worked for him selling drugs. It's awful and all, but Grammy said it best when she heard the news. She said, "The wages of sin is when people do unta you what ya did unta them."

Amen to that.

To be honest there's a lot I don't understand about what happened after the storm, and why some people were so good and full of love and others so mean and hateful. But this much I do know: That day on the bridge I was a proud African American. I was a white kid from New Hampshire. I was my mother's baby. I was my father's son.

I was the one and only Zane Dupree.

The Path of
Hurricane Katrina

MISSISSIPPI   **ALABAMA**

Mobile ●

Biloxi ●

TEXAS   **LOUISIANA**   Gulfport ●

New Orleans ●

Aug. 29
Category 3
Max. wind speed
125 mph

GULF OF MEXICO

Aug. 28
Category 5
Max. wind speed
175 mph

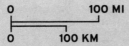

0   100 MI

0   100 KM

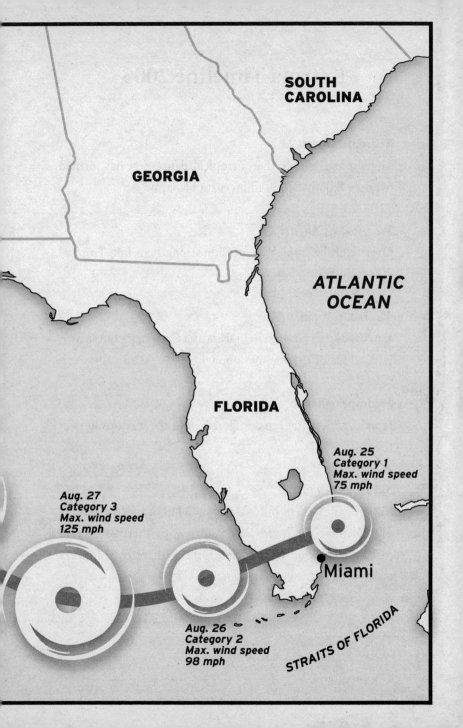

Katrina Timeline 2005

Tuesday, August 23
Meteorologists note that a tropical depression has formed over the Bahamas, 230 miles east of Miami.

Wednesday, August 24
Overnight the tropical depression strengthens into Tropical Storm Katrina.

Thursday, August 25
Katrina makes landfall in Florida as a Category 1 hurricane, with winds of 75 miles per hour.

Friday, August 26
Hurricane Katrina crosses Florida into the warm waters of the Gulf of Mexico.

Saturday, August 27
Katrina strengthens into a Category 3 hurricane, with winds of 125 miles per hour. Forecasters warn that it has a 45 percent chance of striking New Orleans directly. Voluntary evacuation of the city is ordered.

Sunday, August 28
7:00 a.m.
Overnight, Katrina strengthens to a Category 5 hurricane, with winds of 175 miles per hour.
9:30 a.m.
A mandatory evacuation of New Orleans is ordered. Those who can, leave.

Monday, August 29
5:10 a.m.
Katrina makes landfall fifty miles south of New Orleans, with winds of 125 miles per hour.
6:50 a.m.
The system of levees that protect New Orleans from storm surges are breached, swept away like sand castles at the beach. The pumps fail. The Great Flood begins.

Interesting Facts about New Orleans and the Great Flood

New Orleans was colonized first by French trappers and traders, who made encampments among the villages of Native Americans in the area. It was then occupied by the Spanish and later reoccupied by the French before being sold to the United States as part of the Louisiana Purchase in 1803. Over the centuries it has absorbed waves of immigrants of almost every language and ethnicity, including French, Spanish, African, Native American, Haitian, Latin American, Cuban, Italian, German, Jewish, and Asian.

The word *Creole* originally referred to descendants of the French and Spanish settlers. It can also refer to people of mixed race whose ancestors were raised in the complex, racially divided culture of New Orleans.

The people referred to as Cajun are descendants of French Canadians who were exiled from Canada beginning in 1755. They speak their own distinct form of the French language.

Natives of New Orleans have a variety of ways of pronouncing the city's name, among them: New OR-luns, New AW-luns, New AW-lee-uns.

The greater New Orleans region is divided into ten parishes. Parishes are the equivalent of counties.

New Orleans is surrounded by water, with Lake Pontchartrain to the north, Lake Borgne to the east, and the Mississippi River lapping around it from the west and south and east.

The word *hurricane* derives from Hurican, the god of evil of the Carib tribe.

A levee is a deep-sloping embankment of earth and rocks intended to protect an area from floods and storm surges. In the Netherlands similar structures are called dykes. There are sometimes walkways or paths along the top of earthen levees. There are levee systems in many areas along the lower length of the Mississippi River.

Scientists and engineers had warned for years that the system of levees and floodwalls protecting New Orleans suffered from flawed designs and lack of maintenance, and would likely fail if the city were struck by a major hurricane.

The flood that resulted from the levee and floodwall failure during Hurricane Katrina destroyed or damaged more than one hundred thousand homes.

Damage from the storm and flood was in excess of eighty billion dollars.

Nearly two thousand people were killed, many of them trapped in their homes as the floodwaters surged. At least a thousand others may have died from aftereffects of the storm. An unknown number remain missing. Some bodies have not yet been identified.

The Superdome was designated as a "shelter of last resort." City officials were quoted as saying they "didn't want to make it too comfortable" because that would encourage people to stay behind rather than evacuate, which was safer. As a result there was not enough food, water, supplies, or emergency medical care for those who sought refuge during and after the storm.

The American Red Cross opened and staffed more than a thousand shelters throughout the affected regions of Louisiana, Mississippi, and Alabama. However, no shelters were opened in the city of New Orleans in the days immediately following Katrina because the agency did not want to put its workers in harm's way, according to a Red Cross spokesperson. There was also a concern by local officials that a Red Cross presence would encourage newly homeless residents to stay in the area and complicate the recovery efforts.

In contrast, it is the stated business of the United States Coast Guard to go in harm's way. In the hours and days following the flood the USCG saved 24,135 people from imminent danger by helicopter rescue and by boat, and evacuated 9,409 patients from inundated hospitals. It is indisputable that, were it not for their skill and courage, the death toll would have been much, much higher.

Before Katrina, 453,728 people lived in the city of New Orleans. A year later the population had declined by more than two hundred thousand, most of whom left the city because homes or jobs (or both) had been destroyed. According to the *Times-Picayune* it was the biggest mass migration in modern American history.

At one point eighty percent of New Orleans was underwater. The depth exceeded twenty feet in some places. In Biloxi, Mississippi, the tidal surge exceeded thirty feet, killing more than two hundred people and sweeping away thousands of homes.

More than a million Gulf Coast residents were displaced by Katrina. About half were able to return home within a week or two. The other half remained in shelters or temporary housing (motel or hotel rooms) for months.

New Orleans is the busiest port in the United States, with more than six thousand ships and barges passing in and out of the Mississippi River every year. Ships enter the river ninety-five miles south of the city.

As a hurricane, Katrina existed for only 168 hours, start to finish, but a year later more than one hundred thousand displaced people were still living in toxic trailers supplied by FEMA, the Federal Emergency Management Agency.

Deputies Confront Evacuees at Crescent City Connection Bridge

When pedestrians fleeing floodwaters and the chaos of the Superdome attempted to cross the river out of New Orleans, they were stopped from entering the West Bank town of Gretna, and nearby Algiers, by a blockade of police who repeatedly fired shotguns over their heads. Most of those stopped at the bridge were people of color; most of the police were white. The Gretna police chief was quoted as saying, "If we had opened the bridge, our city would have looked like New Orleans does now: looted, burned and pillaged."

Incident at Danziger Bridge

Six days after Katrina, New Orleans police opened fire on a group of unarmed residents attempting to cross Danziger Bridge to seek food and shelter. Four were wounded. Two others were killed: James Brissette, seventeen, and Ronald Madison, forty, a developmentally disabled man who was shot in the back.

Rumors of Chaos

After Katrina, wildly exaggerated rumors of gangs of young black men looting and murdering swept through New Orleans, sometimes repeated by city officials, police, and the media. Armed white militias patrolled white neighborhoods, posting signs that warned *We Shoot Looters*. The *New York Times* quotes John Penny, professor of Criminal Justice at Southern University, as saying, "The environment that was produced by the storm brought out what was dormant in people here — the anger and the contempt they felt against African Americans in the community. We might not ever know how many people were shot, killed, or whose bodies will never be found."

Author's Note

Although this is a fictional account, everything that happens to the characters in *Zane and the Hurricane* reflects real events and situations that affected real people in the days during and after Hurricane Katrina and the flooding of New Orleans. It is one small story, seen through one young man's eyes, and therefore limited to what he directly experienced. It is not the whole story of Katrina — not by a long shot.

I wish to thank all the survivors who took the trouble to record their experiences in many formats and made the information freely available to anyone with Internet access. Those who wish to know more about Katrina are urged to read *The Great Deluge: Hurricane Katrina, New Orleans, and the Mississippi Gulf Coast* by Douglas Brinkley and *Breach of Faith: Hurricane Katrina and the Near Death of a Great American City* by Jed Horne. Their vivid depictions of events helped me get the facts straight, as did many articles in the *Times-Picayune*, the city's fabulously well-written newspaper. And if my facts aren't straight, the fault is entirely my own.

Worthy documentaries include Spike Lee's intriguing *When the Levees Broke: A Requiem in Four Acts* and *Trouble the Water* by Carl Deal and Tia Lessin. Both films contain astonishing footage of the actual storm.

Those who wish to know more about incidents like those that took place at the Danziger and Crescent City Connection Bridges are encouraged to enter the phrase "rumors of looters New Orleans Katrina" into a search engine and see what pops up.

My late wife, Lynn Harnett, read early drafts of *Zane and the Hurricane* and her insights and enthusiasm for the idea were critical to the completion of the story. The comments and suggestions of Bonnie Verburg, my longtime editor, and Dominick Abel, my longtime literary agent, were invaluable. Again, any errors, omissions, or failures are my bad, not theirs.

New Orleans residents Bambi R. Hall and CDR Raymond C. Brown, USCG (Ret.) helped introduce an old New Hampshire boy to the city and generously shared stories about the flood and the aftermath. Thank you.

Zane and the Hurricane focuses on one young man's experience in New Orleans, but Katrina's damage was not restricted to that city. Much of the Gulf Coast was devastated. Whole towns and villages were swept into the sea. No doubt there are many astonishing stories of loss and survival yet to be told, by someone other than me.

Possibly you.

— **Rodman Philbrick**